BETRAYAL *in the* BADLANDS

DANA MENTINK

D0012071

Steeple
Hill®

Published by Steeple Hill Books™

STEEPLE HILL BOOKS

Steeple Hill®

Recycling programs for this product may not exist in your area.

ISBN-13: 978-0-373-44414-4

BETRAYAL IN THE BADLANDS

Copyright © 2010 by Dana Mentink

www.SteepleHill.com

Printed in U.S.A.

Logan stayed quiet for a moment, letting Isabel ease out of her shock. Very slowly he laid his hand on her forearm. "I heard you scream. What happened?"

She tried several times before the words came out. "It was the man, the one who pushed me into the ravine. I went to visit Cassie's grave and he was there, watching me."

Logan frowned. "How do you know it was the same man?"

Her eyes brimmed with tears. "That awful song. He sang the same song."

He kept his voice soft and gentle. "Did he touch you? Hurt you?"

She started to tremble. "No. He just watched me. Watched me run and fall and get up and run again. He just watched me. And..."

"And what?"

Her voice dropped to a whisper. "Logan, he knew my name."

Books by Dana Mentink

Love Inspired Suspense

Killer Cargo
Flashover
Race to Rescue
Endless Night
Betrayal in the Badlands

DANA MENTINK

lives in California with her family. Dana and her husband met doing a dinner theater production of *The Velveteen Rabbit*. In college, she competed in national speech and debate tournaments. Besides writing novels, Dana taste-tests for the National Food Lab and freelances for a local newspaper. In addition to her work with Steeple Hill Books, she writes cozy mysteries for Barbour Books. Dana loves feedback from her readers. Contact her at www.danamentink.com.

Thou hast taken account of my wanderings; Put
my tears in Thy bottle; Are they not in Thy book?
—*Psalms* 56:8

The book is dedicated to readers both near and far who honor me by reading my words and lighten my heart with their kind words of encouragement. Thank you.

ONE

The dead quiet made Isabel Ling's skin prickle. In less than an hour the sun would set and she'd be all alone on this road, a good forty minutes from town and another half hour from Mountain Cloud Ranch. She couldn't stop the thought that rose in her mind as she wrestled with the flat tire. Was it a spot like this where her sister died not three weeks ago? A lizard darted under her truck, causing her to drop the lug nuts.

She chided herself as she retrieved them from the dust. "You're thirty-two years old, Is. Not some scared teenager. No one is going to hurt you here." Gritting her teeth she heaved the new tire from the trunk and began to wrestle it onto the axle, ignoring the ache in her head. It was not the time for another attack. She had nothing else with her, not so much as one piece of hard candy, so going unconscious from her hypoglycemia was not an option.

"Need a hand?"

Isabel yelped and whirled around, losing her grip on the tire. She found herself staring into the tanned face of a stranger. He wore a baseball cap with the Air Force logo embroidered on it. His hair was crew-cut style and his chin shadowed in stubble. Perspiration glistened on his forehead and darkened his tank top. Isabel saw her own scared face mirrored back at her in his sunglasses, until he removed them.

She closed her mouth and lifted her chin, willing her knees to stop shaking. "I didn't hear your car."

He shrugged, breathing hard. "I'm out for a run."

She tried not to gape. "In this heat?"

The green of his eyes were a startling burst of color in his browned face. "Good for the soul. Where are you headed?"

Something about his voice was familiar. She wiped a hand across her brow to buy time. "Mountain Cloud Ranch."

His smile wavered. "Cassie Reynolds's ranch? Are you related?"

"We are—were sisters. I'm Isabel Ling."

"Logan Price." He rested his hands on his hips. "I knew Cassie."

The tension in her stomach grew as the pieces fell into place. "Oh, yes. You called to see if you should finish the work on the ranch."

He looked down for a moment. "I hope that was okay. I didn't mean to bother you. I hate leaving a job unfinished."

He had sounded kind on the phone, with a voice that was uncannily familiar, but she'd suspected that his call was motivated by the desire to be paid for his work. Now here he was, and he probably knew more about Cassie than she did.

Since Isabel had run away from home at sixteen, she had only exchanged six letters with her sister. Six ridiculously small pieces of paper, instead of the volumes they should have shared. She swallowed hard and forced herself to look him in the eye, feeling again a stab of familiarity she could not explain.

He raised an eyebrow. "Are you taking care of Mountain Cloud?"

Isabel shot him a tight smile. "Looks that way. I think I'd better get this tire on."

"Let me help you." He bent to take the lug wrench from her hand, muscled shoulders gleaming in the sunlight.

"No, thanks. I can do it."

"I'm sure you can. I'd be happy to help. You look tired."

Isabel stepped between him and the tire. "I appreciate it, but I don't need help."

He looked at her for a long moment, expression unreadable. "Okay. Do you have a phone?"

She pulled the new satellite phone from her pocket. He took it.

"Nice phone."

"Thanks." She was still smarting over having to buy it at the airport after she lost track of her other one. She wished her checking account total was as hefty as the balance on her credit card.

He punched a few buttons and handed it back, long fingers brushing hers.

"I programmed in my cell number, just in case you need it. I really am sorry about your sister." After another searching look, he turned and ran back down the road, long legs moving easily over the scorched ground.

Isabel watched until he was out of sight. She finished fixing the flat, wondering if Logan knew more than he was telling about things. The suspicious look on his face had been evident in spite of his warm smile.

She brushed the gravel off the knees of her jeans. Maybe he was simply a kind-hearted guy, on a Good Samaritan mission. He could be just what he seemed, her wariness only a product of her past and guilt over not knowing her own sister.

Remember Rawley, Isabel. Remember what happened with him.

She shivered at the thought, the tiny throb in her hand reminding her of the kind of pain misplaced trust can bring. She repeated her hard-earned wisdom again, to cement it more firmly into her brain.

Never trust a stranger.

She recalled the flash of Logan's green eyes.
Especially a handsome one.

Logan ran faster, the sweat pouring off him in a tide of heat. So Isabel was Cassie's sister. He should have known, in spite of the different last names. They both had the same dark hair and delicate Asian features.

His earlier conversation on the phone with Isabel had stuck with him for an inexplicable reason. The honest emotion in her voice when she talked of her sister awakened something in him. He didn't think honesty and emotion went together, in view of his past experiences. He had a divorce certificate to prove it.

While Cassie had been exuberant and impulsive, Isabel seemed different. Maybe it was grief over her sister's accident, but his gut told him it was more. She was scared of something or someone.

He was so lost in thought, he didn't notice the strange play of light until the pain in his ankle forced him to a walk. He froze. A glint, the barest moment of light that shone from the cover of a cluster of spruce trees in the distance. He knew it instinctively. It was the gleam of sunlight bouncing off binocular lenses.

His pulse accelerated a notch, and he had to force himself not to seek cover and get a bead on the enemy.

You're not on a mission anymore, Logan.

When the odd glint did not repeat, he decided it was probably a kid playing, enjoying the last few days of August before school started up again. Still, the tingle of unease remained with him down the mountain, all the way to his truck and during the drive to his condo.

The ungainly pounding of Tank's approach brought a smile to Logan's face when he entered the gated yard. How had this nutty dog twined itself around his heart so completely?

In a way, it was a good thing that Bill couldn't keep him anymore. It was the only positive thing about his friend's extended absence, as far as he could see. The broad-shouldered rottweiler galloped up and threw himself on his back for a belly rub, as if he hadn't seen Logan in months. He tossed the rubber ball for his eager pet. When they lay tired out on the grass, his mind returned to the lonely mountain road.

The standoffish Isabel Ling had arrived as suddenly as a mountain storm. She was wary, reserved, as she had been on the phone, but his unease began before, when he had first arrived on Cassie's property with his backhoe. It was nothing he could point to directly, no outward sign of danger. A feeling had crept up on him as he'd started work, as if someone was watching from behind the trees. Watching and waiting.

His instincts shouted the same message when he'd seen the glint of binoculars earlier.

It must be a by-product of his training, a remnant of the dire situations he'd found himself in during his six years in pararescue. Was it simple paranoia?

He'd learned long ago, on the bloody sands of Takur Ghar, to trust his instincts.

But women were an entirely different breed of danger.

What were his instincts telling him about Isabel Ling? He could sum it up in one word.

Trouble.

Isabel finally rounded the last turn as the sun set, plunging the ranch into eerie darkness. In the distance, towers of rock jutted out like clawed fingers against the sky. She hadn't realized her sister's property was so close to the fabled Badlands. Isabel hadn't ever seen Mountain Cloud, the place Cassie bought after their father's death four years before. She hoped it had been a healing place for Cassie. She deserved it after caring for their father, who had shredded the family into unmendable tatters with his drinking and rage, the horrible depression that gripped him when his business had failed along with his wife's health.

Not completely unmendable, Isabel reminded herself, thinking of the letters. The thought made her throat thicken with tears.

She'd made a stumbling step toward reconciliation after far too many years and Cassie had been receptive, or so Isabel thought. The hope that Cassie had forgiven her desertion lifted Isabel out of the despair that had seemed inescapable. Though Isabel had never forgiven her father, refusing to even keep his last name, maybe she and Cassie could have put the past behind and started fresh.

A tear trickled down her cheek. Too late. Why had she waited until it was too late? The quickening wind drew her back to the present, bringing with it a wall of clouds that seemed to press the air down around her in a hot blanket. Though she should have been exhausted from her flight and the seemingly endless drive, her nerves tingled.

Living in Los Angeles meant being surrounded by people, noise and unending business.

Here there was only the wind rattling the dry leaves and the lonely hum of some hidden insect.

The wood-sided cabin beckoned, and Isabel wanted nothing more than to run inside and lock the door. Instead she dropped her bag on the steps and headed for the corral and adjacent barn. Six horses stood quietly, watching her approach, whinnying softly.

"Hey, fellas. Glad to finally meet you." She let herself into the corral and kept a respectful distance. Her horsemanship skills were rusty, leftover from summers spent at her uncle's place. One thing she did remember was that horses didn't like surprises, especially horses rescued from abuse and neglect, as these had been. Keeping up a steady stream of conversation, she checked to see that the water trough was filled as she made her way to the barn.

She was pleased and surprised to find the barn clean, stalls mucked out and fresh bedding on the floor. It must be the work of Cassie's hired hand, John. A soft snuffle made her start. Off in the corner, almost lost in the shadows, was a horse unlike the others. He was smoke-black with a streak of white between his eyes. A thick mane flowed over his wide shoulders. He danced nervously when she took a step toward him, but did not back away.

"Hello there." She could not take her eyes from the power-ful lines of the horse. "You must be Blue Boy. Cassie sent me your picture." She felt instinctively that he must be the one that had thrown Cassie to her death. She should despise the animal, but she couldn't, not when she knew how much her sister had loved the beautiful creature.

The horse continued to shift around, the straw crackling under his well-tended hoofs. Blue Boy's coat was glossy and smooth, marred only by the scar that circled his front leg. "It looks like someone has been taking good care of you." She held out her hand, fingers outstretched, and Blue Boy allowed a quick stroke to his muzzle. "We'll be getting to know each other better," she whispered as she backed out of the stall, Blue Boy's dark eyes fixed on hers.

The first drops of rain splattered on her face as she exited the corral and hurried toward the house. She wasn't sure how she would get in if the door was locked, but fortunately it swung open under her hand. The interior was dark and sti-fling, as if it hadn't been used in a very long time.

Isabel grabbed her bag and started into the house.

Before she made it over the threshold, a loud flap of wings erupted from the nearby trees as an owl shot out of the canopy with an alarmed cry.

She froze in terror.

It's just an owl.

The thought comforted her for only a moment.

But what was hidden in the silent woods that had startled it into flight?

Hours later, Isabel lay awake, thrashing around in her sister's small bed. It seemed wrong to sleep here, but there was no other bed in the tiny cabin. The wind increased to a howl and rain splattered in angry gusts on the roof. A squeak from outside caused her to sit up, heart pounding.

It's just the weather, Is. Your sister wrote you the summer storms were rolling in.

Cassie's last letter had been chock-full of enthusiasm and even an invitation to visit, peppered with details about an upcoming event in the Badlands. The words were full of life, like Cassie had been. She wondered again. Why had her sister gone riding at night? Had it been a night like this? Wind-whipped and wild?

When the clock ticked its way to 3:30 a.m., Isabel finally threw the covers off and went to the kitchen for a drink of water. Little stacks of Post-its overflowed from a basket on the counter. She prowled the cupboards until she found a glass, noting the pantry was stocked with boxes of cereal, soup and packages of Oreos. She smiled. Cassie had still had the same sweet tooth from her youth. She used to fill her pockets with cookies every day before school.

Isabel felt like an intruder poking through the cupboards, as if she was somehow violating her sister's privacy. Finally she located a glass and filled it. A small window over the sink looked out on the property, moonlight trickling between the thick clouds. Isabel nearly choked as she caught a glimpse of Blue Boy disappearing into the trees.

How had the horse gotten loose?

She didn't take the time to consider, as she pulled on her

jeans and windbreaker from that day and ran into the rainy night, stopping just long enough to grab a flashlight from her backpack. The fence around the corral was open, but a quick head count showed the rest of the horses safe in the barn. Only Blue Boy had made an escape.

Slamming the gate shut, Isabel tried to formulate a plan as she took a bridle from the fence and headed toward the woods. She considered trying to call John, Cassie's hired man, but she didn't have his number and was afraid to take the time to search the cabin to find it. There were no neighbors for miles around.

You're it, Isabel, so figure out what to do.

She gripped the bridle and flashlight more securely. Blue Boy was skittish and they hadn't yet developed trust between them, but somehow she had to find him and convince the animal to be led back home. The rain dampened the August heat, settling the dust and leaving the air crisp and clean. As she plunged into the trees, she wondered again what had startled the owl earlier.

A cold ribbon of fear snaked up her spine. She purposefully shook it off. *No fear, Isabel. Never again.*

She pushed her way past rain-soaked foliage and pine branches that slashed at her face. There was a movement a few yards to her right. She thought she glimpsed the flicker of a mane.

"Come here, fella," she called softly, edging closer to the place where she'd seen him. The trees thinned and the air became cooler. Her flashlight beam picked up only the soaked foliage.

"Where are you, Blue Boy?" She wasn't sure she would be able to see his smoke-dark coat in the gloom. Maybe in the daylight, but if she waited another three hours she might never see the horse again. If she had arrived earlier and scouted out the property she might have an idea of where Blue Boy was headed, but she was on completely unfamiliar ground that was getting more and more uneven the farther she progressed. Gritting her teeth, she edged closer to a pile of rough-hewn boulders.

The wind lifted her hair, whirling it around her face. A sudden gust of cool air hit her and she took another step forward. She felt a presence behind her.

Out of the darkness someone rose up, pushing her forward with a violent shove. Arms flailing, she fought to keep her balance, but tumbled forward.

A loud crack of rock sounded above the wind, and the ground began to move under Isabel's feet. She slid on an avalanche of rock down into a ravine, concealed by darkness and foliage.

Rocks and dirt rained down as she tried to shield her head with her arms. Desperately she dug her feet into the sliding debris, but the effort did nothing to stop her momentum as she was carried along.

With a sudden jolt that shook her to the core, Isabel slammed into a boulder at the bottom. A shower of rock fragments continued to move past her until the rush slowed into a trickle and then stopped.

Her head spun and sparks danced before her eyes. For a strange moment, she thought she heard snatches of a man singing.

The old flag, lovely old flag.

She tried to clear the muddle in her head.

Eyes closed, she took stock. Gingerly she moved her legs and arms, fearful of setting loose another rock slide. Wiping the grime from her face, she discovered she was wedged against the large boulder, her legs buried under a foot of soil and rock. Inch by inch she wiggled her feet, testing to see if anything was broken. A shooting pain up her ankle made her gasp, and she realized with a start of terror that her foot was pinned between two enormous hunks of rock. Try as she might she could not pull it free.

Struggling to catch her breath and control the fear, Isabel looked up toward the mouth of the ravine. It was steep, the top bathed in darkness.

She'd been pushed; there was no mistaking that, probably by the person who had let Blue Boy loose. She could still feel the blow that toppled her over the edge. Someone wanted to kill her, someone who could very well be waiting at the top for her to crawl out. Or maybe on their way down to make sure she hadn't survived.

Her entire body was shaking and she could feel her ankle beginning to swell.

Screaming for help would alert her attacker that their mission wasn't complete, and the chances of a passerby hearing her cries were negligible.

Isabel's teeth chattered and panic flowed through her veins like a strong poison. Hugging herself to try to stop the shudders, she felt the hard surface of the satellite cell phone in her pocket, under a blanket of rubble.

The phone with Logan's number programmed in.

Her heart thudded wildly.

Call Logan.

She didn't trust him, didn't even remember his last name.

He could have something to do with her sister's accident or be covering for the people who knew what had happened to Cassie. He could have been the one who pushed her.

But he'd offered to help her before, his smile gentle and seemingly genuine and strangely familiar.

Trust your instincts, Is.

Instincts? Instincts hadn't helped her steer clear of Rawley Pike. Instinct hadn't helped her at all. Except for one important thing, she reminded herself. That strong urge inside had brought her back to the faith her mother had tried

so desperately to instill in her girls. Should she follow her
heart now?

Trust a stranger?

She clenched her hands together and mumbled a prayer.

Help me trust the right person this time.

Biting her lip until she tasted blood, Isabel dialed.

TWO

Logan jerked awake at the ringing of the phone. He was instantly alert, ready to ship out on the next mission, until the present rushed back in again. Four in the morning and he didn't recognize the number on the caller ID. He made a move to roll over and ignore it, but turned and snatched up the receiver in spite of himself.

"Logan."

He couldn't hear an answer, only the crackle of a bad connection and the word that had always given him purpose. "Help."

He recognized the voice, fear running deep through her words. "Isabel? Where are you? What's wrong?" She whispered her predicament. He got the gist of it; just enough to know her location and that she didn't want a rescue crew. "You need an ambulance."

Her words came through forcefully this time. "No. Just you." There was a pause. "Please."

He heard her difficulty in uttering the last word and understood. He'd never been good at asking for help either. "Stay put, don't try to move. I'll be there as soon as I can."

Then he was throwing on clothes, grabbing some essential supplies and racing to the truck, with Tank thundering behind. On the way up the mountain, he pushed the vehicle as fast as it would go and thought about Isabel's half-crazy chatter. Something about Blue Boy and a stranger in the woods. She said she'd been pushed into a ravine.

Logan pressed the accelerator harder. Pushed? She'd probably gotten confused, alone on a strange property before sunup. Still, the twinge of unease he'd felt before began again. He shook it off as he crested the last ridge before Mountain Cloud Ranch.

It was still dark but the rain had eased off, turning into a soft mist that enveloped him as he headed for the rocky end of the ranch, Tank at his heels. There was no sign of Blue Boy or anybody else as he pushed through the greenery and found the edge of the ravine where there was clear evidence of a recent rock slide. He lay belly down on the edge and called into the darkness.

"Isabel?"

"I'm here." The relief in her tone was palpable.

"Are you hurt?"

"I banged up my ankle. It's caught between some rocks and I can't get free."

"I'm coming down. Hold tight." He told the dog to stay as he fastened a rope around a sturdy spruce and looped it through the carabiner on his belt. Shouldering the backpack, he began the backward descent into the ravine. Each step was precarious, causing the rock to move and shift. He paused often, fearing his progress would shower more debris on her.

Sweat poured down his face in spite of the cool. He shouted to her frequently, keeping her talking, warding off shock, or so he hoped, and giving him a direction.

Finally his feet touched bottom and he unfastened himself from the ropes. He switched on a flashlight and made his way quickly to her.

Her face was pale in the dim light, coated with grime. From

what he could see, her pupils were even and reactive when he flicked the light across her field of vision. He knelt next to her and felt her wrist. "Hey there. This is a crazy way to explore the property."

She didn't smile. "I was after Big Blue, and someone pushed me."

He could feel the pulse in her wrist begin to race. It was not the time to get into that. "Let's focus on getting you out of here. I'm going to give you a quick check, with your permission."

She nodded, lying still as he ran his hands along her arms and legs. He gently slid his fingers along the back of her neck. "Any pain? Numbness? Tingling?"

"No. Are you a doctor?"

"I'm a little of everything." He pulled out a pry bar from his backpack and circled around behind the rock. "When you feel the rock move, pull your ankle free. Can you do that?"

"To get out of here I could do anything."

He chuckled and leaned his weight on the pry bar. It shifted, but not enough. He added more force behind it until his muscles screamed at the effort. Finally the rock slid just enough that Isabel pulled clear.

He scrambled around the rock and found her crouched over her ankle, fighting against the pain.

"One obstacle down. How about we see to that ankle now?" It was swollen and bruised, but not misshapen. A good sign. "Could be you got out of this with a bad sprain." He wrapped the joint as gently as he could with a bandage and activated a chemical cold pack to sandwich between the layers of bandages.

She was sitting up now, eyeing him with an expression he couldn't decipher. "Logan, did you…hear singing up there?"

He shot her a look, checking to see if she was slipping into shock. "No, ma'am. Must have been the wind."

"I guess so. I got really mixed up when I fell. I don't even know how long I've been down here." She watched him finish the bandaging. "You seem like you do this kind of thing every day."

He felt the dull twinge of pain. "I used to. You ready to get out of here?"

She nodded and he helped her to stand on her good ankle. Then he refastened himself to the rope. "Can you carry the backpack?"

When she nodded, Logan slid the straps onto her shoulders and began to fasten a webbed belt around her waist before he pulled her tight to his back. He felt her stiffen when her chest touched his shoulders.

"What are you doing?"

Her breath was warm on his neck. "I'm getting us out of here. I'll do the climbing, and you hold on. Deal?" Without waiting for an answer he began hauling them up out of the ravine, Isabel holding him around the waist, her head pressed to his shoulder.

She didn't make a whimper of complaint as they climbed, even when he could not avoid banging into the jagged rocks. Her repaired ankle throbbed, and her dead weight on his back made the going rough.

It didn't matter.

It could have been two hundred feet or two hundred miles.

He would finish the mission.

Gritting his teeth he pulled them along, hand over hand, until they reached the top of the ravine. With a whine of joy, Tank grabbed hold of Logan's sleeve and yanked for all he was worth.

Logan hauled them both over the top, unstrapped Isabel from his back and helped her to sit. Tank darted from Logan to Isabel, licking them both.

"This is Tank."

She smiled and rubbed him under the chin. "Good name."

"Good dog."

The sky had lightened from black to gray to pearl as the sun pushed its way toward the horizon. They sat in silence for a while, Logan trying to catch his breath and Isabel staring at him.

He gave himself a few more moments to recover and then got to his feet. "We need to get you inside. How about another piggyback ride?"

She shook her head. "I can walk."

"You'll damage your ankle further."

Her eyes shifted and she chewed her lower lip. "I can't let you carry me anymore. You've got to be exhausted after that climb. I'll hop on one foot, if you can steady me."

He put on the backpack and wrapped an arm around her shoulders. She clung to him to keep from falling. As they struggled for balance, Logan glanced down at the wet earth near the edge of the crevice they had just emerged from.

Isabel followed his gaze. "What is it?"

He shrugged and moved them in the direction of the cabin. "Later."

With Tank at their heels, they set off.

It was only a half mile back, but it took them almost a half hour to hobble along. Finally they pushed through the door, and Logan deposited Isabel on the small couch in the front room, where Tank promptly curled up in an untidy pile at her feet.

Logan fetched some ice from the freezer, wrapped it in a dish towel and laid it on her ankle.

"I'll drive you to town for an X-ray."

"No. It's just a sprain. I don't need an X-ray."

"Yes, you do."

She pressed her lips together. "No."

He sighed. "Are you always this stubborn?"

There was a glimmer of a smile on her face. "I'm afraid so." She fiddled with the edge of the blanket he'd draped over her shoulders. "I—I want to thank you. You don't even know me, but you came over here in the middle of the night and hauled me out of that hole. I still can't believe it happened."

He looked directly into her ink-dark eyes. "I can."

She blinked. "You believe me? That I was pushed? Why?"

He chose his words carefully. "Because there was a set of footprints in the mud at the edge of the ravine, someone wearing cowboy boots."

"Could they be your prints?"

He shook his head and pointed to his feet. "I'm in mountain climbers. Whoever made those prints stood right at the edge, and watched you fall."

Isabel stroked the dog as she drank the instant coffee Logan prepared for them both, trying to calm herself. It was almost 7:00 a.m. by now. She wasn't sure what to say to the man who had gone to such trouble and physical torture on her account. She could tell by the far-off look in his eyes that he was trying to make sense of the past few hours, too. She felt a familiar trembling and tried to get up.

Logan laid a restraining hand on her shoulder. "Stay put. Whatever you need, I'll get it."

"I—I need something with sugar."

He eyed her closely. "Diabetes?"

"Hypoglycemia. I haven't eaten regularly since I came."

He went to the kitchen and returned with a handful of Oreos for her and one for himself. "So what made you come to the ranch?"

"Cassie loved her horses. I wanted to make sure things were taken care of, until the property can be sold."

His eyes bored into hers. "You don't want to live here?"

She shrugged. "It isn't my property. I figure Cassie probably left it to my uncle, and I don't really have fond memories of South Dakota anyway."

"Been here before?"

"Yes," she said grimly.

Logan didn't question further. "Okay. Change of subject. Let's talk about who would want to shove you over the edge of a ravine. Did you upset anyone recently?"

Upset anyone? One person sprang to her mind immediately, a certain ex-husband who was still languishing in jail, thanks to her. She looked at her hands.

Logan folded his arms, his voice low and serious. "You don't have to talk to me about it, but the cops are going to ask you the same thing, so you might want to have an answer ready for them."

She started. "The cops?"

He leaned forward. "If someone just tried to kill you. You need to file a police report."

The thought of facing the barrage of personal questions that was sure to follow made her stomach turn. "Maybe it was some crazy person and he's moved on."

"You and I both know that's improbable." He hesitated before he finished. "Whatever happened might be related to your sister's accident."

Isabel's mouth fell open. "You think there's something strange about my sister's death, too?"

He held up his hands. "I didn't say that. It just occurred to me that Blue Boy could have been spooked by a stranger on the property the night he threw Cassie."

"My sister grew up around horses. She wouldn't have been thrown easily."

"I agree with you, and I've thought about that quite a bit.

She managed Blue Boy, and he's a handful. It never made sense to me why your sister took off riding at night."

Though she was relieved to have someone else voice her suspicions, the idea of bringing it all up to law enforcement fanned the anxiety in her gut. There was no other choice. If she wanted the police to look more closely at Cassie's death, she needed to tell them what had happened. "I guess I'll talk to the cops."

He put down his coffee mug. "I'll drive you to town right now."

"You don't need to drive me. I can…"

He pointed to her ankle. "I'll drive."

Before she could fire off a retort, Tank got to his feet and barked, pressing his wide face to the window. Logan pulled back the curtain. "Well, there's one bit of good news, anyway."

Isabel hopped over as Logan opened the front door.

A stocky man in jeans and a flannel shirt was dismounting Blue Boy. Two other people on horseback hopped down from their saddles, too.

Isabel couldn't suppress a cry of joy at the sight of the horse. "Blue Boy. I didn't think I'd see you again."

The stocky man shrugged. Isabel guessed him to be somewhere in his midthirties.

"Found him running loose on our property. I know he's Miss Cassie's horse." He extended a hand. "I'm John Trigg."

"Isabel Ling. My sister mentioned that you worked for her."

He tipped his cowboy hat. "Yes, ma'am." His eyes narrowed. "I've been taking care of things. I figured if Cassie had any family they would more than likely sell the property."

Isabel didn't miss the hint of petulance in his words. Instead of answering, she smiled at the other two people. A heavy-set man with a florid face stroked his mustache and stepped up onto the porch. "Hello, Ms. Ling. I'm Carl Trigg, John's father."

"And the mayor." Isabel shook his hand. She smelled a trace of whiskey on his breath. "My sister told me you helped her a number of times. You own the adjoining property."

He chuckled. "Sure do. It's been our oasis from the political storm for years. Nothing like being out in nowhere to make you remember what's important. This is my wife, Sheila."

A blonde lady with shoulder-length hair extended a hand and clasped Isabel's palm in hers. "Pleased to meet you. We were so fond of your sister." Her eyes shifted to Isabel's foot. "What happened? Have you had an accident?" She turned to Logan. "And this handsome soldier came to your rescue, I suppose?"

Soldier? That might explain Logan's arsenal of rescue skills. Isabel invited them in, and the mayor and his wife settled next to her on the couch. Logan leaned against the door. John excused himself to return Blue Boy to the barn.

Mayor Trigg cleared his throat. "So tell us what happened, young lady."

Isabel gave them a quick overview.

Mr. and Mrs. Trigg's eyes grew increasingly wider until the mayor leaned forward.

"Somebody pushed you? Who would do that?"

Sheila frowned. "And why?"

Logan raised an eyebrow. "That's the question of the day. I'm going to drive to town so Isabel can talk it all out with the police."

The mayor nodded thoughtfully. "Absolutely. Mountain Cloud is a pretty quiet town and we like to keep it that way. Let me know if there's anything I can do to help."

Sheila caught Isabel by the arm. "I'm going to have John bring over some supper later. You shouldn't be standing in the kitchen with a bum foot."

"Oh, please don't go to any trouble. I'll be fine."

Sheila laughed. "It's not trouble, it's being neighborly. That's what people do here." She pulled a card from her purse. "And here's Carl's business card. He never remembers to hand them out himself, even now that he's running for the Senate." She took a pen from her small waist pack and scribbled on the back. "Our home phone and my cell number, just in case you need it. We're about a half hour east of here as the crow flies, but the road is twisty and steep."

The overflow of concern made Isabel flush. She'd tried and succeeded at keeping to herself since her disastrous marriage had ended a decade earlier. Ten years of hiding in shame. It felt strange to be thrust into the middle of a community that returned lost horses and made dinners for others. She took the card and thanked them again.

When the rattle of hoofbeats died away, Logan helped Isabel to his truck. He stopped Tank from careening into her lap.

"Hey, buddy. You're riding in the back this time."

Logan started the engine and they drove off the property. As they did so, Isabel caught a glimpse of John closing the corral gate. The hostility on his face was clear in the look he gave them.

Cassie may have trusted the man, but something in his look told her to be careful.

Very careful.

THREE

Logan eyed Isabel as she sat on the hard-backed chair at the tiny police station, waiting to talk to an officer. When her turn came, he gave her a reassuring nod. "I've got to pick up an order. Tank and I will meet you back at the truck when you're done. You okay to walk?"

She nodded. "Yes, my ankle's better. I think the swelling's gone down."

He felt reluctant to leave, but he forced himself out of the building. Tank fell into step next to him. Logan could not shake the instinct that told him something was wrong. The watcher in the trees? His own unease when he'd started working on Cassie's ranch?

Maybe, just maybe, it was the result of being close to a lovely woman again. Could a woman still have the power to unsettle him? As he quickened his pace toward the print shop, he felt the familiar pain build to a wall inside, stoked by the thought of how gullible he'd been, how stupid. It was as if he could hear Nancy's revelation about the baby word for word in his mind. The baby that wasn't his. The marriage that had never been enough. The world tilted in that moment, throwing off his equilibrium. He'd stumbled through months, years, after that, never quite recovering his balance. He ignored the pain in his ankle, aggravated by his effort to help Isabel, and moved quicker down the hot sidewalk, Tank panting behind him.

He wondered what the police would make of Isabel's story. *Stay out of it. She can fight her own battles.*

Carl Trigg pulled to the curb and got out of his truck. "Logan. How's Isabel? Thought I'd better come and check on things. Still can't believe someone would have pushed her." He raised an eyebrow. "Do you think that's what happened?"

"I thought she might have imagined it at first, but there were fresh footprints on the edge that didn't match mine or hers."

The mayor's brow crinkled and he let out a sigh. "I'll make sure it's investigated fully. We can't have this sort of thing going on." He hooked a thumb in the pocket of his pants. "Sheila wanted me to talk to you about a job. Gonna put up some fences, but the ground needs to be cleared first. Your schedule open?"

Logan's face warmed. "Your son could do that job fine, Carl. You don't need to pay me to do it."

Trigg waved a hand. "John wants to spend every waking moment in the stables. No time for fences. We're indulging him until he puts that law degree into practice. Got distracted by Cassie Reynolds and her horses."

"How's he taking it? Cassie's death."

"Oh, well, he was sad, of course. He respected her and they shared a common passion for horses, but that was about it. We're all saddened about that girl's accident. Sheila's even decided to help Isabel plan a nice memorial service, if she wants. We want to help, you know. Speaking of help, we've got business with you. How about that fence project?"

Logan cleared his throat. "Look. I know you and Sheila are trying to help me make a success of this business, but you've done enough by loaning me the start-up money. I'm going to get this thing on its feet and pay you back."

He smiled. "Sounds like you're on a mission. Okay, I'll tell Sheila, but she won't be happy."

Logan returned the smile. "Tell her I'll stop by next time she makes one of her berry pies."

"I'll do that." Carl waved and got back in the truck.

Logan hurried toward the shop to pick up the promotional flyers he'd ordered. If he didn't start booking some jobs soon, he would be hard-pressed to live up to his words and all the flyers in the state wouldn't make a difference. The knowledge that the mayor and his wife were offering charity work to tide him over left a bitter taste in his mouth.

Saving the business should have been the only thing on his mind, but he couldn't resist a quick look back at the police station.

When Isabel was finally ushered back to meet Officer Bentley, she felt only uncertainty deep in the pit of her stomach. After a deep breath, she settled herself into a chair across from the whip-thin officer and took the offensive. "Hello, Officer Bentley. We spoke on the phone when you called to notify me about my sister."

His dark eyes showed no expression. "I remember. A bad call to have to make."

"Yes. I know you think Cassie's death was an accident." She sucked in a deep breath. "Maybe after you hear what happened to me last night, you'll think differently."

He listened, pencil poised, while she related the bizarre episode. After a long look, he put the pencil down. "Ms. Ling, are you sure someone pushed you? Isn't it possible you stumbled and fell? In the dark, and on that property, it would be easy to do."

Her cheeks warmed. "I didn't fall. Someone shoved me and maybe that person had something to do with Cassie's accident, too. There are footprints there. Whoever did it wore cowboy boots."

He sighed so deeply the breath fluttered the corners of his mustache. Isabel could see threads of silver in his hair. "You can't throw a stick around here without hitting someone wearing cowboy boots. I'll be happy to ride up there and check it out, if that would ease your mind."

"But you don't believe me?"

"People experience grief differently. Sometimes it's easier to imagine there's someone or something to blame. Your sister was thrown from a horse. If you want to affix blame, you can pin it on Blue Boy. Some of those horses your sister rescued had been beaten, hurt bad. You never can really heal an animal like that."

She willed her voice not to crack. "I'm just presenting facts to you, Officer Bentley. Please listen to me."

He sat back in his chair, the lights accentuating the creases in his forehead. "All right. Let's say you were pushed. My next question is, who do you know that would like to see you at the bottom of a ravine?"

Isabel swallowed hard. "I—I have an ex-husband named Rawley Pike who believes I wronged him, but he's in prison in Orange County."

The officer's eyes narrowed slightly. "I'll check on that. Can you tell me the date he was incarcerated?"

She drew in a breath. "August fifth, ten years ago."

He raised an eyebrow. "And the crime?"

"Dealing drugs. Cocaine and heroin. And he killed a man during a deal that went bad."

"You turned him in?"

Her skin prickled all over. "Yes, I turned him in."

"I'll check on his status."

And that means he'll find out everything about you, too. She nodded weakly. "The footprints?"

"As I said, I'll take a look and if there's something there, we'll talk about it more. Right now, I've got a meeting."

He rose and led Isabel to the door.

She wandered out into the blaze of late-morning sun, her stomach still churning. He didn't believe her and, what was worse, he was now going to look up her whole sordid past. Logan had not returned to the truck. A sign on the building next door revealed it to be the office of Dr. Lunardi, the person who had examined Cassie and pronounced her dead. He'd also helped Isabel make long-distance burial arrangements.

Isabel walked gingerly to the small building. A white-haired receptionist looked up from her keyboard. "May I help you, honey? Did you need to see the doctor?"

She felt suddenly flustered. Why had she come in? Her face flushed and she fought the desire to run out the door again. "Er, yes. I think I sprained my ankle. Could Dr. Lunardi take a look?"

The lady consulted the computer screen. "He's got a few minutes. Come on back."

She led Isabel to an examining room and went to fetch the doctor. A short while later Dr. Lunardi appeared, a small man with the dome of his head shining and smooth and a fringe of neatly trimmed black hair in a semicircle around his scalp.

"Hello, Dr. Lunardi. I'm Cassie Reynolds's sister. You were so kind to help me make arrangements for her."

He dropped his pen and bent to pick it up. "Ms. Ling. I didn't realize you were her sister, with the different last names."

"I took my mother's maiden name."

He fiddled with some papers on a clipboard. "Should have seen the resemblance. I was happy to help you with your sister. I can point you to the right people to plan a memorial service, too, if you wish."

"I would like that very much."

"Wanda says you've had a tumble. May I take a look?" He busied himself prodding her ankle.

"Dr. Lunardi, I wondered if you could tell me about Cassie, when they brought her in. John Trigg found her, didn't he?"

The doctor nodded, but didn't look up. "Yes, John called the rescue squad and they transported her here because…" He cleared his throat. "Well, I'm sorry to say it, Ms. Ling, but there was no hope of resuscitation. I pronounced her dead."

"From the head trauma?"

"Yes."

Isabel turned the thought over in her mind. "Was there anything unusual about it? Anything that struck you as odd about my sister's injuries?"

"What?" He blinked. "No, not unusual. Why would you ask such a thing?"

Isabel sighed. "I wondered if there was something that I don't know about."

He stiffened. "Your sister was thrown by a horse and died of head injuries sustained in that process. That's all there is." He pointed to her ankle. "It doesn't appear to be broken or fractured. Continue to ice and keep the Ace bandage on to help you get along until the bruising heals. If it's not better in a few days, come back. Now if you'll excuse me, I have other patients. No charge for the visit today. Welcome to town, Ms. Ling."

He hurried out of the room.

She rewrapped her ankle with the bandage and left the exam room. Wanda was not at her station and there was no sign of the doctor. The heat enveloped her immediately as she left the air-conditioning behind. Across the street, a cool spot of wooded green beckoned her. She wasn't sure if she was ready to face it, but she knew she had to try.

Heart pounding, she made her way to the cemetery.

Cassie was buried here, the arrangements made long-distance as Isabel had struggled to scrape up enough money to fly here to South Dakota. Somehow she would have to come up with the cash to pay the bills when her credit card came due and to plan a beautiful memorial service for her sister.

There would be flowers and sweet music and someone to sing the old hymns like their mother had done when they were children.

Tears pricked her eyes as she entered the cemetery. Trees shrouded it from the road and the quiet was broken only by the twitter of birds. The headstones were well tended, the grass trimmed and many were dotted with small tokens or flowers from loved ones. Isabel walked slowly until she found her sister's grave.

Cassie Reynolds.
Child of God.

What things would she have had written on the stone if she had known her sister better? Lover of horses? Willing servant who cared for their abusive father? But maybe *willing* wasn't the right word. Cassie took on the role because Isabel had run, abandoned her family and left it all behind for her sister to deal with after that final, awful confrontation with their father.

The tears left hot trails down her cheeks.

"I'm so sorry, Cassie. I was weak and selfish and I waited too long." She ran a hand over the grass that surrounded the stone. "Why didn't I reach out earlier?" It was a question she had asked God almost continually since she had gotten the phone call three weeks prior. The grief squeezed her heart so hard she thought it would stop beating. "I wasn't there to help when you needed me. I wasn't even there to bury you properly. I'm so sorry."

Sitting under the trees, alone with her sister, she let the sadness flow.

It could have been a few seconds or many minutes before

the sound sank into her consciousness. An eerie, familiar tune that took her a few moments to place.

"The dear old flag…"

It was the strange song she'd heard right before someone had pushed her into the ravine. She leaped to her feet, whirling around. The song continued in soft, low tones.

She backed up against a wide pine and scanned wildly for the singer.

Finally she spotted him, standing in the shadows, leaning against a headstone. He was thin, dressed in brown pants and a tunic, slouch hat over his long reddish-blond hair. His eyes were pale, icy and metallic, as he stared at her.

Her mouth went dry and she could not force out a word. Her gaze slid down to his feet.

Cowboy boots.

With a graceful gesture, he tipped his hat and gave her a wicked smile. "Afternoon, Isabel."

Logan didn't see Isabel at the truck, so he stopped in the grocery store. He didn't need anything in particular, just killing time, but he came out with a bag nonetheless. Tank got up from his spot in the shade and greeted his owner with typical canine enthusiasm. Logan gave him a scratch behind the ears and loaded the supplies into the truck.

Still no Isabel.

He scanned every inch of the sun-soaked street. If she was still in with the police, he decided, things must not be going well. It wouldn't hurt to drop in and check. He was headed in back toward the station when he heard the scream.

He took off at a dead sprint for the direction of the cry; the cemetery. Tank raced along beside him, matching him stride for stride. His mind took note of certain facts as his body hurtled along. Unfenced area. Cover from trees and shrubs.

Plenty of places to take a shot, hide an assailant, conceal a body.

He gritted his teeth and crouched as he ran through the entrance, staying low, his route zigzagging as he scanned for any sight of her, or signs that there had been a struggle. He stopped to listen, sweat beading on his face.

Tank gave him a questioning look.

He quieted his breathing and listened again. This time Tank took off on his own, darting from headstone to headstone, moving steadily up the slope.

Logan ran after the dog until he heard it. The tiniest of noises, a shuddering hiccup. He headed for the sound, body still low, feet soundless as he could make them. It took him only a moment to find her.

Isabel was crouched in a ball behind a gravestone, her face stricken with terror.

When Tank bounded up, Logan commanded him to sit.

"Isabel." He reached out a hand to her and she jerked back violently, breath heaving, eyes unfocused.

"Don't touch me," she hissed.

He knelt next to her. "It's okay. It's Logan. Remember me? Logan Price. I drove you up here."

Her face was blank, frozen in fear by whatever had caused her scream. He called Tank to his side. "Remember my dog, Tank? He's been looking for you."

When Logan released him, Tank trotted up to Isabel and licked her face. She jerked at first and then wrapped her arms around his neck, pulling him close, her fingers clinging to his black fur.

Logan stayed quiet for a moment, letting the dog ease Isabel out of her shock. Very slowly he laid his hand on her forearm. "Can you talk now?"

She looked at him for a long time before she blinked,

rubbed the back of her hand over her eyes and nodded, all the while keeping one arm around the dog.

"I heard you scream. What happened?"

She tried several times before the words came out. "It was the man, the one who pushed me into the ravine. I came to visit Cassie's grave and he was here, watching me."

Logan frowned. "How do you know it was the same man?"

Her eyes brimmed with tears. "That awful song. He sang the same song."

He kept his voice soft and gentle. "Did he touch you? Hurt you?"

She started to tremble. "No. He just watched me. Watched me run and fall and get up and run again. He just watched me. And…"

"And what?"

Her voice dropped to a whisper. "Logan, he knew my name."

He squeezed her forearm, wishing he could force the fear out of her. "Stay here. I'm going to check around."

She looked panicked, so he added quickly, "Tank will stay with you. No one will touch you when he's on duty." He ordered the dog to stay and moved away.

He did a quick perimeter check and worked his way inward in ever-diminishing circles until he rejoined Isabel. "No trace of anyone."

She was calmer now, but her voice still held an edge of panic. "He was here. I saw him. Leaning right against that tree. I'm not making it up."

Logan reached out a hand to her and, after a moment of indecision, she took it.

"We're going to go back to the police station, and this time, I'm staying with you."

FOUR

Isabel hardly registered the walk as Logan took her by the arm and guided her back to the police station. She expected to see the leering face of the crazy man from the cemetery behind each tree and bush. All of her nerves were alive with residual fear. When she recoiled at the snap of a branch, Logan kept her moving forward. He was outwardly calm, but she could tell he was monitoring the surroundings as they made their way to the station.

The only thing that kept her moving was the pressure of his strong hand holding hers and an occasional nudge from Tank's wet nose. Some distant part of her mind questioned Logan's concern. He was a stranger, looking to finish work on her sister's ranch. She didn't know a thing about him, really.

Except that he'd climbed down a cliff to get her.

And shown up at the sound of her scream.

She tried to see some sign of his feelings on his face, but there was only a look of concentration there, a man doing his job.

What was Logan's job, anyway? The Triggs indicated he was military, but he'd had time to do construction work for Cassie and come to her aid twice. Was he home on leave?

In a few minutes she found herself sitting in Officer Bentley's office again, facing his disbelieving stare. If Logan hadn't been standing next to her, she would have run for the door.

The officer looked at Logan before he gestured for Isabel to talk.

"I went to the cemetery and…" Fear closed over her again, her throat thick with tears. It was the same terrible fear she'd tried to put behind her since she'd sent her ex-husband to jail. She'd kept it tamped down, rolled into a dark corner of her heart, but it was back again, a jagged emotion that cut through her insides.

Logan finished the story as best he could.

Officer Bentley made more notes. "Did you see the guy, Logan?"

"No."

He turned back to Isabel. "Could you identify the man if you saw his picture?"

She nodded. "I think so."

He led her to a sparse room with an older model computer.

"Probably got a faster way to do this back in L.A." He asked Isabel for a basic description of the man—race, age range—and pulled up a series of pictures on the screen. "Start here and keep going until you find a match or run out of pictures."

She thought there was a hint of derision in his voice as she took her place at the computer. Logan sat down next to her.

Bentley switched on a fan, which turned feebly in the stuffy air. "I'm going to check out the cemetery. I'll be back shortly."

The door swung closed behind him with a sharp bang.

Isabel looked at Logan. "He thinks I'm making this all up."

Logan sighed. "Maybe, but he's a good enough cop to check things out anyway."

"Do you think that, too? That I'm making it up?"

His green eyes bored into hers. "I believe you were honestly terrified in that cemetery. I also think that's not an unfamiliar feeling to you."

Her cheeks warmed. "So you wonder if I might have dreamed up this guy because I've been in bad situations before?"

"You didn't imagine the footprint next to the ravine. I saw those myself."

She tried to read the feeling under his words. Skeptical, yes, but not dismissive. And for some unknown reason, he was doing his best to help her out. She couldn't figure out a logical motive, so she applied herself to scrutinizing each picture. An hour later, she'd only made it through a couple hundred mug shots.

"This is taking forever." She looked around and found a notepad by the phone, along with the stub of a pencil. She sketched quickly until she got the essence of the man who had terrorized her. Long, thin face, pale skin, gray-blue eyes, long, reddish hair and the faintest hint of a goatee on his chin, a felt hat pulled down over the forehead.

Logan watched over her shoulder as she drew, his hard shoulder touching hers. Pulse quickening, she handed the sketch to him.

He whistled. "You are one talented artist."

She felt her face warm again. "A hobby of mine, since I was a child. That's the guy."

He sat down again. "He looks like some kind of soldier from the past."

A shock went through her and she gasped. "That's it."

"What?"

"The song. He was singing a song about a wounded drummer and the flag. It made me think of an old soldier of some sort."

Logan looked closer at her sketch. "This man isn't old

enough to have fought in anything but maybe Desert Storm and Iraq. Let me make a copy of this and we'll leave one with Bentley. With your permission, I'd like to send this along to a friend of mine. He may be able to help us ID the guy."

She nodded and turned back to the pictures as the song played in her mind.

Logan drummed his fingers on the steering wheel as he drove back to Cassie's ranch. Bentley hadn't returned to the station before they'd left, but another cop had been there to take the sketch. No one in the database matched Isabel's description of the man. "I'm sure the guy's gone, but maybe you should consider staying in a hotel in town. Just for a few days."

Isabel shot him a frightened look, then raised her chin, brushing the long strands of black hair out of her face. Her voice was soft but determined. "Thank you, but I'm going to stay at my sister's ranch."

He eyed the worn patch on the knee of her jeans. "If it's a matter of cost, I could…"

She cut him off. "No. Thank you, I'll be fine."

He'd offended her. Even though his offer was meant to be helpful and it was the most logical solution, she was annoyed. He wanted to apologize, but he didn't. Talking just made things worse, started arguments, raised the level of conflict. Things were so much easier in pararescue. You went in. You saved people and hopefully didn't get killed in the process. Not one of his saves had ever objected to his methods. He sighed.

You're not a pararescueman anymore, Logan. You're a regular guy who doesn't understand women. Welcome to the club.

They drove by a group of workmen erecting a section of raised bleachers on the sidewalk.

Isabel watched the progress as they passed, stroking Tank's head where he'd shoved it through the small cab window into the front seat. "What's going on?"

He was relieved to have the silence broken. "Getting ready for the Moonlight Ride. It's a big event to fund the horse rescue efforts in and around this town. They start with a parade and end with a night ride through the Badlands. Your sister…" He knew as soon as he said it, it was another stupid topic. *Bring up the girl's dead sister? Great, Logan.* "Lots of locals help out with the festivities."

Isabel peeked around Tank's head. "Was Cassie going to be a part of the event?"

He sighed. "Yes. She was working with some of her horses, getting them in shape to take participants on the ride. She was passionate about her rescue work, but you know that already, I'm sure."

Isabel ducked her head and stared at her hands. "Yes."

He tried to keep the conversation going. "John was helping her acclimate the horses to the saddle. They'd ride together at night sometimes."

Isabel's head jerked up. "Was he with her when she died?"

"No. She took a horse out on her own. Seemed to be heading for the Badlands when she was thrown. John found her when he came to the ranch the next day before sunup and discovered Cassie and Big Blue were gone." He shifted. "Listen, I'm sorry to bring up your sister. I know it's painful for you."

She shook her head. "It's okay. I want to know everything about my sister's life."

And her death? Logan had thought the circumstances of Cassie's last night were strange, but he had dismissed it, until Isabel had come into town. The two encounters with the singing stranger almost convinced him something might be suspicious after all about Cassie's death. But maybe the strange events had more to do with Isabel's past than the present. He looked at her profile, the dark hair like a shadow against her porcelain skin, the delicate almond shape of her eyes that spoke of an Asian ancestor. He wondered if anything would ever erase the fear that he'd seen on her face in the cemetery, the way she'd pulled from his touch as if his fingers burned her skin. Who had hurt this woman? And why did the thought of it make him grind his teeth?

He shook off the feeling and rolled down the window, letting the blast of air barrel into the truck with enough noise to make conversation impossible as they began the climb up the mountain road.

The ranch was bathed in afternoon sunlight when they arrived, a palette of amber and bronze. To Logan's mind it was the perfect place, quiet, away from tourists and traffic, with the spectacular Badlands jutting into the sky behind, as if they could stand guard somehow. He wished they could. The twist of uncertainty remained in his gut as they got out of the truck, Tank jumping down to join them.

The horses nickered softly in the corral. Isabel stopped at the fence to stroke the silky coat of the nearest one. Her hands were tiny and delicate against the wide muzzle of the horse. She laid her head against the animal's for a moment. Logan had the strangest notion that he'd seen her before, long ago.

The mixture of loss and frustration on her face made him take a step forward. Should he try to comfort her? Ignore her pain?

She took a deep breath and pulled away from the horse.

To give himself something to do, he grabbed the brown bag from the truck and handed it to her.

"What's this?"

He was surprised to feel his face flush. Blushing? He

hadn't blushed since grade school. "Some supplies. In case you run low."

She reached in and extracted a package of Oreos. Her laugh was soft and silvery. "Thank you. I think I'll carry them around in my pockets, like my sister used to do."

He chuckled. "Better not. You'll have a herd of horses following you everywhere."

She looked thoughtful. "Thank you, Logan. For everything. It was a lot for you to do for a stranger, and I appreciate it."

Her words sounded as though they'd been pulled out, one by one, painfully presented. "Don't mention it. You've got my number in case you need anything, right?"

He could see her gathering herself, subtly straightening up to tell him she wasn't going to need help. They were interrupted by the arrival of Sheila Trigg in a silver truck. She got out and fetched a container from the backseat.

"Hello, all. John couldn't be bothered to bring over a casserole, so I did. What's this I hear about some lunatic bothering you at the cemetery?"

Logan saw the look of surprise on Isabel's face. "Nothing stays secret very long here."

Sheila moved with them toward the welcome cool of the house. "We've never had anything like this happen in our town before, that I'm aware of. Are you sure you didn't bring this trouble from L.A.?" She laughed as she slid the food into the fridge, but Logan didn't miss the momentary look of horror that crossed Isabel's face before she composed herself again.

Whatever trouble she'd had in L.A. was certainly no joking matter.

Sheila turned to them again. "Listen, I know you're probably tired and overwhelmed but I wanted to let you know that John will continue to help you with the horses for as long as you need him. Also, I wanted to offer to help you plan a memorial service for your sister. It's hard not knowing anyone in town and, let me tell you, there isn't a soul here I don't know. I'd be happy to help you with the planning."

Isabel's voice caught as she answered. "That would be very kind."

Logan wondered if she was concerned about how to pay for a service. He'd not missed the worn clothing and her beat-up suitcase, too small to hold much of anything.

Sheila continued. "And everyone will understand if you back out of Moonlight Ride."

"Back out?"

"Well, your sister committed to taking a group out on her horses that night and helping with the meet and greet. Don't worry, though. We can round up more horses from somewhere, I'm sure."

Isabel was about to answer when there was a knock at the door. Logan answered it.

Officer Bentley tipped his hat and smiled at Sheila. "Afternoon." He turned a look on Isabel. "Nothing out of the ordinary at the cemetery. Came to photograph the footprints. Can you show me where they are exactly?"

Sheila joined the party as they headed into the hot afternoon. She kept up a lively conversation. Logan was used to her irrepressible personality and was happy to let her fill the strained silence.

Isabel walked next to him, shoulders tense and a worried frown on her pale face. She scanned the trees every so often, eyes wide. He hoped she wasn't heading into another blood sugar plunge. He should have stopped to get sandwiches in town, or a soda at least. In this heat…

There you go again, Logan. She's not your responsibility. Just get this done and go home.

Sheila chattered on. "Your sister had big plans for this place. She wanted to clear the ravine and restore the creek that ran through here, make it a real sanctuary for the horses. I admired her ideas, but I'm sure glad I wasn't having to foot the bill or the back work to get it done." She laughed and wiped the sweat under her fringe of blond bangs.

They approached the ravine and he felt the cooler air rushing up at him. Bentley readied his camera as they pointed out the spot where she'd gone over the side. They formed a semicircle and peered closely at the ground.

Logan went down on his hands and knees. The moisture left by the previous night's storm had disappeared, leaving the ground hard and dry. The footprint would be nicely preserved.

Officer Bentley was silent for a moment. "Sure this is the spot?"

Logan ignored the irritation that flared inside him. "Yes. I'm still pretty good at pinpointing locations."

Bentley grunted. "No offense meant. I'm just not seeing any footprints here."

Logan straightened and shot a look at Isabel. "I'm not either. Someone has wiped them away."

FIVE

Even an hour later, Isabel could still feel the earth shifting beneath her feet, as if the ground was being washed away, worn into precarious gulleys like the massive twisted hoodoos of the Badlands themselves. The prints, the only things that might convince Officer Bentley she wasn't crazy, were gone. If Logan hadn't confirmed that he'd seen them, she would have begun to doubt her own sanity. And the look he gave her as he left to scout the property with Bentley, half worried, half incredulous, made her even more confused.

Should she think of Logan as an ally? But why should he be? They'd only spoken once on the phone before she'd arrived. Suppose he was part of the conspiracy, if there was one? In cahoots with whoever had pushed her and rubbed out their footprints?

Then why would he bother climbing down to rescue you? And above all, where do I know him from?

Sheila Trigg interrupted the tumble of thoughts by handing her a plate with a ham sandwich and some potato chips, followed by a glass of iced tea. She sat down next to Isabel at the table and patted her hand.

"Oh, honey, you look just wiped out. Eat something, at least."

Isabel tried to choke down a few bites of sandwich under Sheila's watchful eye. "Thank you."

"Don't worry about it. I don't know what's going on here, but we'll help in any way we can. You know that, right?"

Isabel sighed. She'd never even met her neighbors in her apartment building, never wanted to, but there was a strange comfort in having people looking out for her in this place where everything seemed new and dangerous. "You've been a big help already. And John has, too. As soon as I figure out how Cassie left things, I'll see that he gets paid."

Sheila waved a hand. "Oh, John would work for nothing if he could be near those horses." She smiled wryly and lowered her voice. "And truth be told, I think he had a bit of a crush on your big sister."

Isabel swallowed. "Really? Were they...dating?"

Sheila laughed. "No. John was never much with people and he's been gun-shy since his last girlfriend moved away without leaving a forwarding address. If I know my son, he probably never worked up the courage to so much as buy her a cup of coffee. Just as well, since he's going to start a law practice at the end of the summer."

Isabel didn't comment, but she wondered if her sister had had any attraction for the stolid John Trigg. She ate a few more chips. "Can you tell me more about the Moonlight Ride?"

Sheila raised an eyebrow. "I didn't think you'd be interested in the details. We figured you were going to pack up the ranch and sell it as soon as you could."

Isabel looked down at her plate. It had been her plan since the moment she'd pawned her gold chain to scrape up the money to fly to South Dakota. Settle Cassie's estate, somehow carve out enough money to give her a proper memorial service, and leave South Dakota behind. Permanently.

It's still the plan, Isabel. You don't belong here. You never did. "I just wondered about it. Logan said Cassie was involved."

"It's an event sponsored by Range Rustlers. They're a rescue group for unwanted horses. Your sister got several of her horses from them. They're hoping to raise enough to buy some pastureland to keep the severe cases until the animals can be tamed enough to find homes. Talk to Bentley if you want to know more. That's his hobby when he's not the long arm of the law."

She thought about her sister's passion for horses, born of early visits to their uncle's South Dakota farm. Cassie'd been fascinated, entranced, and from that moment she'd saved every dime to buy herself a horse.

Isabel remembered the day she'd found Cassie sobbing because she'd used her hard-earned savings to bail their father out of jail after his arrest for drunk and disorderly conduct. Anger kindled to life inside her, followed by the cold lick of shame. Her father had hurt them, but how had Isabel's abandonment injured her sister?

Sheila started and looked down at the cell phone clipped to her belt. "A message from Carl. I've got to go to town and help him with the Ladies Guild meeting. If I don't show up to rescue him, he'll never get out of there."

Isabel followed Sheila to the door. The woman wrapped her in a hug. "I meant what I said. If you need anything, you just shout."

Isabel thanked her again. As Sheila drove away, Isabel scanned the trees for Logan and Officer Bentley. There was still no sign of them. She closed the door and locked it for good measure.

The house was cool, the spruce branches overhead sheltering it from the sun. Isabel wandered through the kitchen and the small bedroom, soaking in the details of her sister's life. A bookshelf crammed with books, mostly about the care of horses. Pictures of Cassie with Blue Boy and one that made her breath catch. It was a family photo, old and starting to fade. Cassie stood next to her father, dwarfed by his tall form, and Isabel smiled from the circle of her mother's arms. She'd forgotten that there was a time when they were a normal family, before her father's business failed, before the alcoholism took over, before her mother's lupus began to siphon her life away. Her eyes blurred. She replaced the photo.

When her body began to tremble she took a few of Logan's cookies and sat on the worn rocking chair to watch out the window for the two men's return. A scrap of white crammed between the cushion and the chair arm caught her eye. She pulled out a folded piece of paper.

> *Dear Isabel,*
>
> *I was really thrilled to get your last letter. My mind began to imagine all kinds of things, how you would come to visit me here and we'd be sisters again. We have a lot to talk about, don't you think? I was furious at you for a very long time. That's why I didn't answer your letters for a while. I thought you had taken the easy way out, running away and leaving me to deal with Dad. From the bits and pieces in your letters, I understand that your choice cost you more than I could ever imagine. I know Dad hurt you badly and, if it matters, I think he was sorry for that. At the end, he asked about you sometimes. Remember what Mom used to read from Matthew? Pray for those who hurt you. I was amazed that she could do that in the face of how he treated her, but she did forgive him, Is. That's what I tried to remember when he was at his lowest. Mom forgave him and prayed for him right up to the day she died.*
>
> *What's that saying? It's water under the bridge*

*now. I have an amazing life here with my horses. I had
a developer approach me about selling. They want to
build a resort here for backcountry types. I've even
had an offer much closer to home, but I've got other
plans. I'm going to have the ravine cleared out and
hopefully it will revert to a natural running creek again.
Logan is doing it for me. He reminds me of Blue Boy,
so proud and trying to learn a whole new life, after his
wife and everything. You've met him before, you know.
I'll explain later. With his help, I'm going to make this a
preserve where people can come and learn about horses
and take trail rides into the Badlands. I'm looking into
having trailer hookups so folks can "camp and ride."
What do you think? A pie-in-the-sky dream? Wouldn't
be the first time. Remember when we decided to open
our own circus? A three-ring circus run by two little
kids. Ha! Maybe I've finally gotten old enough to run
after the dreams before they run away from me.*

*It's getting dark now. I've never been afraid of the
dark before, but lately…well, John just laughs and says
there's nothing in the dark that can hurt you any worse
than the daytime. Still, I find myself keeping the light
on at night, as if there's something out there waiting to
get me. Funny, because you were always the one that
had to have a light on in the dark! I guess I've talked
long enough. I want you to make plans to come see me.
We've wasted too much time already. I've got to go find
a stamp or this will never get to you.*

*Love,
Cassie*

Isabel pressed her cheek to the paper, her breath burning in
her lungs. The precious words. They could have been sisters
again. Real sisters. The notion eased her agony for a moment.

Cassie had moved beyond the anger and the blame. It was a sweet breeze of comfort against the storm of grief and regret that billowed through her. Why hadn't she made those plans? If she'd come earlier, maybe Cassie would never have gone off on that ride.

If she could have followed her mother's advice and forgiven her father...

Her tears dropped onto the paper clutched in her hands.

It seemed as though the flimsy scrap held the weight of her sister's dreams and her own sorrow and shame. The burden was too much. She shot to her feet.

She had to get away, settle things in South Dakota and leave, before she lost herself to the same grief she'd felt at her mother's death. That grief had started it all, the plunge into anger and recklessness that had dropped her at Rawley's feet, kept her in self-imposed exile for all those years. She shivered, tucking the paper securely in her backpack, mind whirling.

John would take the horses, she was sure. From all accounts he loved them. Perhaps the Triggs would even be interested in buying the property. At the very least, she knew Sheila would help her find a real estate agent and do what she could. Logan, too.

The thought of him stopped her.

Proud and trying to learn a new life.

What had happened to his old one?

And when had she met him before?

Logan stood in the shade of a twisted spruce where Tank sprawled on his side. The dog was tired from chasing every unfortunate bird that chose to land among the shrubs. Bentley continued his methodical search of the soil at the edge of the ravine, but Logan knew that was a waste of time. There weren't any prints. He knew it, Bentley knew it. The search was more to assuage Isabel and Sheila. The rain might have blurred the footprints into nothingness, but something in his gut told him it wasn't so.

He pulled out his satellite phone and called his law enforcement contact Bill Cloudman, filling him in quickly. "I'm going to fax you the sketch Isabel drew."

"What makes you think I can shed any light here?"

"Because you know this part of the state inside and out." There was a long silence. Logan knew Cloudman was trying desperately to forget his time as a Tribal Ranger and the death of his young partner. He didn't want to add to the pain, but Bill was the only person he could think of to ask for help.

"I'll take a look at the sketch and poke around a little. Not much to go on. No prints, just the girl's story. You sure she's telling the truth?"

"No, but my gut says there's something to it."

"Trust your gut, Logan. It'll keep you alive."

Isabel, too, he thought as he disconnected. Picturing her dark-eyed intensity brought him back to his youth, growing up in the shadow of the Badlands where life could be as harsh and unforgiving as the land itself. The sizzle of memory rippled through him, a horse stuck in the mud, eyes rolling in terror, imprisoned by the iron grip of the earth, fear shuddering through every muscle and sinew. He wondered why the desperation of that moment stayed with him all these years.

The sound of an engine pulled him from his thoughts.

Bentley looked up too, frowning as Carl Trigg got out the passenger side of a sedan. Logan didn't recognize the driver as he exited, a well-dressed man who looked exceedingly out of place on the wide stretch of graveled driveway. He was further surprised to see the man open the rear door and help Sheila out. Why had she returned so quickly?

Bentley hooked his thumbs on his gun belt, watching the trio make their way to the house. Sheila waved and gave them a "come here" gesture. Bentley muttered something under his breath and walked toward the house.

Logan puzzled as the group was ushered into the house by a startled-looking Isabel. Well-dressed guy had to be a lawyer, probably here to help Isabel dispose of the property. She would sell to the first person to make an offer, no doubt. He'd make the same choice himself. Maybe the Triggs would snatch up the property and let John run things. Just as well. Isabel didn't belong here, she'd said so herself.

He pitched a rock and sent it bouncing off the rough bark of a twisted pine. Tank looked at him as if to say, "I'm tired. If you want that fetched, do it yourself." There wasn't anything to be gained by sticking around. He had the description to fax and plenty of reasons to start drumming up some construction business.

A plane sliced through the blue sky above the property and the longing ignited, intense as it had ever been. The need to belong again, to have a reason to get up in the morning, the team that he would live and die for.

Maybe the pararescue instructor position would pan out.

Not maybe. When. It wouldn't be the same, but he'd still be a part of a unit, a man with a purpose.

Nothing to do about that but wait until his application was considered and his ankle fully rehabbed.

The other alternative crept into his mind. He could go back home to his family's business, a sprawling complex of quarries just begging for a son to take the reins. But spending his days ordering payroll sheets and poring over equipment manifests was a fate to be avoided at all costs. He shook the thought away and forced his feet into motion.

On the way back to his truck, he stopped at the corral to watch the horses. They stood in the sun, tails swishing, unconcerned about being watched, except for Blue Boy. The big horse fixed Logan with a curious stare, unmoving except for the twitch of a muscle in his front foreleg.

"What are you thinking about, big guy?" He could never really know an animal fully. This massive creature, two thousand pounds of muscle, had thoughts and desires that a human couldn't understand. They were complex and sometimes unpredictable, just like people. He was grateful he only had to care for a nutty dog who ate potatoes off his kitchen counter and shredded pillows if given the opportunity.

A movement from the house drew his attention. Framed in the front window, Isabel sat in the same chair where he'd deposited her after he'd pulled her from the ravine. The black hair hid her features but her posture was stiff. Carl stood next to her, a puzzled frown on his face.

He looked at Tank, who was busily sniffing every square inch of the fence. "Thirsty, boy? It wouldn't hurt to stop in the house for a quick drink."

Before he had a chance to reconsider, he tapped on the cabin door and entered. All four people stared at him. "Just wanted to get the dog a drink of water, if that's okay. Sorry to interrupt."

Isabel's eyes were huge, her arms folded across her chest as if she was trying to keep herself in the chair. She opened her mouth to speak, but said nothing.

Sheila, looking a bit startled herself, patted a spot next to her on the sofa. "We were just going to come out and get you anyway, Logan."

He raised an eyebrow. "Me? Why? What's going on?"

The well-dressed man cleared his throat. "I gather you are Logan Price. I'm Doug Barnes, Cassie's attorney. Ms. Reynolds hired me a few months ago to handle her estate. I'm here to go over the details with the involved parties."

Logan tried an easy smile. "I'm just here for a drink of water."

"No, Mr. Price. You're involvement goes far beyond that."

SIX

Logan felt as if he'd stepped onto a movie set. He stood uneasily in the doorway. Tank trotted over to Isabel and flopped down on the floor next to her. She shot a look at Logan that showed her to be as confused as he was. How could he possibly be involved in the reading of Cassie's will?

She was an acquaintance, no more. He recalled a strange conversation when Cassie had hinted that they'd met each other in years past, but they'd never gotten around to finishing the discussion.

Barnes cleared his throat and slid on a pair of half glasses. "This won't take long. I came as soon as I heard you were in town. Ms. Reynolds provided for disbursement of her assets in three ways. First, she wished a sum of ten thousand dollars to go to the Trigg family to thank them for their kindness and continued support."

Sheila bit her lip, blinking against the tears that shone in her eyes. Carl touched her shoulder. Though it was very slight, Logan saw her stiffen under his caress, her mouth tightening for a moment before he took his hand away.

The lawyer shuffled through a few more papers. "The house and property she has left to Isabel."

Isabel jolted as if she'd received an electric shock, her hands flew to her mouth. Tank looked up to see what had interrupted his scratching.

Logan was puzzled. It was her sister, after all, so why the shock at inheriting the property? Yet he'd not seen Isabel visit, not heard Cassie mention her sister more than once or twice.

"There's a message for you, Miss Ling. Cassie writes in her will,

> *'We both made mistakes and unfortunately we didn't get the time to heal them in this life. I know you may want to sell the property. That pains me, but I understand your choice. All I ask it that you hold on to it long enough for Logan to see to good homes for all the horses. Love to you, sis, Cassie.'"*

Logan stared at the lawyer. "Did you mention my name in that?"

"Yes, Mr. Price. The last part of the will pertains to you."

"Me?" He felt the eyes of everyone in the room on him and tried to cover for his shocked tone. "I didn't know Cassie that well."

"I gather she knew you better than you'd think."

"How do you mean?"

He took out the last paper from his portfolio. "Cassie has left you her horses with the stipulation that if you do not wish to keep them, loving homes be found for each one. There is a fund to care for them while they are on the ranch." He looked at Isabel. "She further requests that the horses be allowed to remain on this property while Mr. Price goes about securing adoptive homes for them."

Logan and Isabel gaped at each other. He was too surprised to get a word out.

The lawyer hadn't finished. "There is a note from Cassie on this point as well.

> *'Isabel, I knew it would be too much to "saddle" you with the property and the horses, if you'll excuse the pun. I left them to Logan for a very good reason. Remember Buckwheat? Now take a good look at Logan again and you'll know why I left the horses to him. It took me a while to figure it out.'"*

It took all Logan's power of control not to grab the papers from Barnes's hands and read them for himself. How had he just inherited six horses? It was a mistake. He'd never heard of Buckwheat, and he hardly knew Cassie Reynolds or her sister. He looked over to see Isabel staring at him, a look of shocked wonder on her face. "What is it? What does it mean?"

She stared for a moment longer before she stood abruptly and shook her head. "I need to get some air." Tank dashed after her into the late afternoon sunlight.

Barnes packed up his papers and shook hands with the Triggs and Logan. Carl walked him out and Sheila took Logan's arm. "We never expected anything from Cassie. I didn't imagine she even had two dimes to rub together, poor girl. I was surprised when Barnes saw me in town and asked me to come along."

"Tell me about it." His head was still reeling.

Sheila eyed him carefully. "What was all that business about Buckwheat?"

"I have no idea, but I'm going to find out." He dropped a quick kiss on her cheek and went in pursuit of Isabel.

He caught up with her in a shaded hollow. Moisture sparkled on her cheeks, taking some of the charge out of his approach. "Sorry to intrude. I can come back later if you want to be alone."

"No. We should talk. I'm sure you're wondering."

That didn't cover half of it. He came closer and leaned against a tree.

Isabel talked as if she was speaking more to herself than him. "I hardly knew my sister. I ran away from her, from my family, and left her with all the problems. I just came to this town to give her a proper memorial. I figured the property would go to our uncle or the Triggs. They were like family to her. They would know what to do with it."

"I'm sure they'll help you figure it out. The Triggs are good people."

She nodded absently. "I feel like I'm in some sort of bad dream."

"You don't want the property?"

"No. I don't want to stay here. I want to go home to L.A., and now I've got a house and land to deal with...."

He bit back a surge of irritation. "And I've got a half-dozen horses. Talk about a surprise."

She blinked, as if awakening from a dream. A smile spread across her face. "You don't remember Buckwheat, do you?"

"No. Should I?"

"Not really. I didn't catch on until Cassie's letter."

"Catch on to what?"

"You were young, seventeen maybe. I saw you when you brought him back. I should have realized right away."

Logan jammed his hands into his pockets. "I'm lost. Fill me in."

"We were staying with my uncle at his ranch. Cassie, my mother and me. Mom was sick with lupus, but that didn't stop her from taking Buckwheat out every chance she got. That day, the day it happened, a storm was threatening and it had been raining on and off for weeks. Buckwheat was desperate for a ride, so Mom took him out. The trail was wet and the ground gave way. She..."

Logan closed his eyes as the memory flooded in. "She and the horse fell into the creek and the horse got mired down in the mud."

"You remember now?"

He sighed. "Yes. Your mother wouldn't leave that horse, even though she was freezing and bruised. Neither of us had a phone."

Isabel's lip trembled. "And you promised my mother if she would get herself to safety you would stay with that horse until he could be gotten out."

He remembered the way the lady clasped his hands in hers, the ice cold of her small fingers. After he'd helped her climb out, he'd returned to the frigid water, knee-deep in the muck, and stayed with the animal until Isabel's uncle and two other men finally arrived to pull them both out.

He found Isabel staring at him. "The horse was too traumatized to be moved in a trailer. When I walked him back to your uncle's ranch, you were there, weren't you? Watching me from the barn." The picture snapped into focus. He remembered her stricken face, dark eyes wide with gratitude, hair swirling around her face like smoke. She was, quite simply, the most captivating thing he'd ever seen. She'd taken a step toward him and he recalled the feeling of wanting nothing more than to join that dark-eyed girl in the shelter of the barn, but he'd been ushered into a truck instead and delivered home. By the time he'd summoned up the courage to go back, Isabel's family had gone away.

Isabel sighed. "Yes. I wanted to thank you then, for what you did. My mother would have stayed there with Buckwheat if you hadn't helped her."

"Was your mother okay?"

She looked at her hands. "She came down with pneumonia. She died two months later."

"I'm sorry."

"Me, too." She waved a hand. "For all of this. I know you don't want those horses."

"I'm not in the rescuing business anymore and horses aren't really my thing."

She stood. "I'll find another way, keep them here until I can find homes for them."

He shook his head. "I will honor what your sister wanted. I'll come up and tend to them for as long as it takes." He couldn't believe he'd said it. How was he going to care for a bunch of horses? Especially if...*when* things worked out with his plan to return to duty?

Isabel looked at him thoughtfully. "I understand. You've done so much already." She came to him and threw her arms around him.

He was startled by her hug, her face grazing his cheek, the slender form that fitted so well against his.

"Thank you again," she whispered in his ear.

He was not sure whether she referred to his care of Buckwheat or her. A trickle of electricity coursed through him as she let go.

"No problem. I should head home and fax your sketch to my friend Bill. You've got my number if you need anything. Looks like the horses are bedded in for the night. I'll come by tomorrow." He tried to stop the sudden flow of words by giving her a wave and starting for the truck.

He opened the door for Tank and used the opportunity to cast a look back at Isabel. She stood, small in the tall shadow of the trees, eyes shimmering with emotion.

He remembered the longing he'd felt when he'd returned Buckwheat years before.

For a split second, he wondered what would have happened if he had gone to talk to her in the barn that rain-soaked day.

* * *

Isabel was too tired that evening to do more than drink a glass of milk and collapse onto the bed. A tabbed journal tucked behind the bedside lamp drew her attention. It was filled with Cassie's cramped handwriting: each section held the history of the horses stabled in the barn. She read for a while, until the stories of cruelty and neglect began to overwhelm her. She determined she'd give the volume to Logan to help him find good homes for Cassie's beloved animals. The last thing she remembered was uttering a prayer for Logan to complete the task that had been thrust upon him.

She woke the next morning when the sun poured through a gap in the curtain. Stiff and disoriented, she managed a hot shower and a plate of scrambled eggs, which revived her. She took some Post-it notes from the basket and a pen. The first task was looking into possible new homes for the horses so Logan could be relieved of his burden. John Trigg was probably the best source of information on that.

She went in search of the business card Sheila had given her to request John's number. Phone in hand, she moved to open the curtains in the front room, throwing them wide.

She should have felt the warning prickle. The sense that she was not alone.

She didn't realize the danger until it was too late.

With a strangled cry, she leaped back, intending to run down the hall to the back door.

The long-haired man sat in an armchair, shotgun resting on one knee, slouch hat on the other. "Stay a spell, ma'am," he said, gesturing to the chair with the gun.

Run, run, run! her body screamed, yet she found herself unable to move. "Who are you?" Her voice was a forced whisper.

He pointed again with the gun. "Sit down. Do let us be civilized."

She sank into a hard-backed chair.

He smiled. "Good."

"Who are you?" she repeated.

"You can call me Autie."

"What do you want with me?"

"You are a woman who doesn't waste words. So many women prattle on about nothing at all. It is wearisome." His voice held the gentle drawl of the South.

Isabel thought about running for the door, but she knew he'd put a bullet in her before she reached the threshold. She stayed silent, trying to think of a better plan, heart thundering in her chest. "What do you want?"

He watched her for a while, pale blue eyes glittering under delicate brows. "In perfect truth, I want you to disappear."

The fear leaped in her gut. "Why?"

His long hair shone coppery blond in the morning light. "This isn't the place for you. The Badlands is rugged country. Why, even General Custer found it a challenge." He laughed, the sound soft and high.

She found the courage to answer in spite of the trembling that shuddered through her. "I have the right to be here."

He blinked. "Right? I find it odd that you speak of rights. You ran away. You ran from your family and left your father to die."

Isabel felt as if she'd been slapped.

He fixed her with a stare. "That is the problem of the truth, is it not? You can run across the globe or climb the highest mountain." He glanced toward the stark horizon. "Even this place, these endless Badlands, cannot help you escape your own truth. It will hang around your neck like the heaviest of stones."

He was insane. The chill in his eyes told her he had killed before and he would not hesitate to do so again. He'd already tried by pushing her into the ravine. "How do you know about me?"

He raised a shoulder. "A soldier always does a good deal of reconnaissance before he goes after a quarry. That is how you discover your enemy's weaknesses." He pointed at her. "You lack courage and commitment. You ran when you were sixteen and you will run again."

How did he know so much about her life? Who could have told him? A sickening realization dawned on her. "Did Rawley send you?"

The man's expression didn't change. "I understand he could be getting out of prison soon. Is it not reasonable to think he would want his wife to return home to him?"

"No. No, no. I'm not his wife anymore. He'll never get out of prison."

Autie's jaw clenched and he stiffened. "That is an uncharitable answer, ma'am. Perhaps you are experiencing guilt about sending him to the penitentiary? A man in a cage is no man at all. You might have done him a favor and killed him instead of having him locked up like a rabid dog." His fingers gripped the gun until the knuckles whitened. "A cowardly act which will not go unpunished."

Her mind whirled. "Rawley doesn't want me back." She swallowed hard. "If he gets out, he can start a new life."

"Nevertheless, you need to leave, go back to Southern California."

Isabel pressed her knees together to keep the terror from overtaking her. She could not think of any way to save herself from this madman. "So if I go, you'll leave me alone?"

He shrugged. "I will finish my mission regardless of your choices."

"Stop talking in riddles. What mission?" she snapped.

He looked slightly startled at her outburst. "I see you have more spirit than I gave you credit for. Very good. It will make my assignment all the more enjoyable."

She hissed out the words. "What will happen if I don't leave here?"

"Then, Miss Ling, I will be happy to make you disappear."

Her nerves screamed in terror.

He stood and walked over to her chair until his knees grazed hers. He was so close, his breath stirred the hair around her face. She froze, curled in a knot against the worn upholstery. He let the gun trail the length of her arm. "And you will join your poor sister in the family grave. Then you will be with your father at last." He lowered his voice to a whisper. "That is quite an irony, is it not?"

He laughed, raised his hat and tipped it before he put in on and disappeared out the back door.

SEVEN

Logan faxed the sketch to Bill Cloudman after he returned from his morning run. He busied himself doing the dozen or so chores he'd put off during the week. There was still no word on his application for the pararescue instructor position when he checked his e-mail for the third time. He gritted his teeth and whispered the prayer again. "Lord, You know that's the answer for me. Let it work out."

Pararescue was his destiny. It had been burned into him with every drop of his uncle's blood that had coursed through Logan's fingers as he'd watched the man die, thrown from a horse into a fence. The helplessness he'd felt at that moment stayed with him until age sixteen, when he'd found his calling as soon as he read the pararescue motto: *So that others may live.* A lifetime later, he'd been living out that calling until the accident that shattered his ankle. The acid memories surfaced again and he prowled around to shake loose the darkness, but the new thought that emerged in his mind didn't soothe him.

Isabel was alone with a ranch she didn't want and a bunch of horses that had somehow become his responsibility. He thought about the feel of her arms circling his shoulders after the reading of the will. Something about her intoxicated him, as it had the first moment he'd seen her standing in the barn all those years ago.

He blinked and refocused on the necessary points. The horses needed homes. He had to make that happen before his instructor job was approved. There was no room for failure on either count. First order of business was to get the facts together, any information that Isabel might have to help him place the horses. Then maybe an ad? An Internet posting on the Range Rustlers Web site? With no more than a vague urgency to do something, he grabbed his keys and left the condo.

On the way to the truck, he passed the backhoe tucked neatly into the side yard, secured on its trailer. He'd never finished clearing the ravine as Cassie had directed him. She'd paid him a deposit and he'd only just begun when she died.

An unfinished job.

Understandable in view of the circumstances.

Completely understandable.

And unacceptable.

With a sigh, he hitched the trailer to the back of the truck.

Tank scrambled in the driver's side and they headed toward Mountain Cloud Ranch.

It was already in the nineties when he pulled into the drive at a little after nine. He was surprised to see the front door of the cabin open. Instincts pricking, he got out and jogged toward it, the dog at his heels.

"Isabel?" He heard no response and he started to run. As he crossed the threshold, he crashed into Isabel as she hastened out of the house with a battered suitcase in her hand. They went down in a pile of arms and legs and came to rest with her still clinging to the suitcase, pinning his legs with her body. She immediately jumped up, the baggage like a shield in front of her. Tank pranced around, alternately pushing his wet nose against Isabel's pant leg and head-butting Logan.

"Are you okay?" Logan avoided another sloppy lick from the dog and got to his feet. "Sorry I knocked you over. I saw the door was open and it looked like something was wrong."

Her eyes were wild. "Something is wrong. That crazy man was here, in the house, with a gun."

Logan gaped. "What?"

"He knows all about me and he said if I don't go back to L.A., he's going to make me disappear."

Logan took her wrist and felt the pulse hammering double time. He led her to a chair and she sat, still clutching her suitcase.

"The same man from the cemetery?"

She nodded, lips quivering. "He knows I ran away when I was sixteen. He knows about my father. He's on some sort of mission. I think he works for Rawley."

"Rawley is…"

She looked at the floor. "My ex-husband. He's in prison because I turned him in for drug dealing."

"You think he's after revenge?"

She shrugged. "Probably. I know some of the things he did to people who crossed him." She shuddered, tears suddenly filling her eyes. "I thought that chapter of my life was finally closed. He's been in prison for years. Why is he after me now?"

"We'll go to the police again."

"No." She shook her head. "They can't do anything. I'm leaving here. I'm sorry to stick you with the horses. I'll figure out with the lawyer how to deed the property to you and when you sell, you can use the money any way you want."

He started to protest, but she cut him off.

"He says his name is Autie and he knows I ran out on my family. He knows everything."

Logan saw the years of grief and guilt buried in her eyes. "And he knows just what to say to injure you the most."

She sank back in the chair. "Yes. He's making me a victim again. Just like Rawley did."

He wanted to ask more about Rawley, but the defeat in her face stopped him. "Where will you go?"

"Back home. I'll close up my apartment and then I'll find someplace else."

"Do you have any family you could stay with for a while?"

She bit her lip. "My uncle and I don't talk. Cassie was my only family."

They were silent for a moment. Logan replayed the events in his mind—her fall into the ravine, the stranger at the cemetery and now this close encounter. He had not laid eyes on the stranger who stalked her. Bentley had implied maybe it was all in Isabel's head. Instinct told him she was telling the truth, and that same instinct made him want to do something about it. "Before you do anything, let's talk to Bentley again and check in with my friend. He may have some info that could help us. Just sit tight for a minute."

When she didn't answer, he pulled out his phone and called Bentley, who wasn't in the office. Logan left a message indicating he'd stay with Isabel until Bentley could join them, and then he texted Bill Cloudman to call him immediately.

While he sent the message, Isabel went outside and began to pace along the corral fence. Blue Boy shimmied back and forth on the other side, his feet stirring up the dry dirt, until he stopped abruptly and stuck his long neck over the rail to gently nuzzle the top of her head.

Logan's phone buzzed and he clicked it on, watching the powerful horse as he did so.

Blue Boy was restless. If only he could talk and tell him what he knew of the man who was intent on terrorizing Isabel Ling and perhaps shed light on Cassie's death, as well.

Isabel stayed stone still, feeling Blue Boy's warm breath on her hair. It was the gentlest of touches before he dropped his head to stare into her eyes. She caressed him, trailing her fingers over the silky coat and strong lines of his proud face.

Cassie's notes on Blue Boy came back to her.

He'd been bought as an investment, left in a rented stall and ignored, ridden infrequently by the overworked staff at the stable that boarded him. When the owner grew tired of the expense of upkeep, he took Blue Boy far out into a desolate wooded area and left him. The horse was found months later, miles away, his right foreleg trapped in a length of barbed wire that cut down to the bone. Blue Boy was emaciated, weakened by infection; the vet believed the kindest thing would be to euthanize the animal.

The Range Rustlers called Cassie and she took him in.

Isabel looked down at the faint scar circling his front leg.

Unwanted.

Lost and alone.

Rescued.

Saved.

She'd been all of those things, too. But one thing she'd never faced before was the responsibility for another creature as cruelly treated as herself.

She looked back at the little house that her sister had loved and again at the group of horses silently regarding her with uncertainty in their postures. Rawley had taken her need and vulnerability and used it to make her a victim. Once more she reached out a hand to Blue Boy and he touched his whiskered lips to her fingers.

Her tiny mother would have faced up to anyone or anything that threatened her loved ones. She'd stood between her raging alcoholic husband and her children with only a spatula in her hands and her faith that God would give her the strength to defend them.

But you didn't stand up, Isabel. You ran away, from your family, from Rawley.

Her breath grew tight in her chest and the resolution filled her like the roaring of a strong wind.

"I won't leave you," she whispered to Blue Boy. "Not until you find a good home. I will not abandon you like I did my sister." She tasted the saltiness of her own tears. "I promise."

Blue Boy whinnied in reply.

Wiping her face, she prayed. *God, help me keep my promise.*

The noise of an engine startled her. She watched Logan ease the backhoe off the trailer and park it in the shade of the trees.

"What's that for?"

He shrugged. "Cassie paid me to clear the ravine and the job isn't finished. I'm going to be here anyway working with the horses, so I'll complete the project. It might help you sell the place." He looked away for a moment. "Will you leave me your number? So I can touch base with you when the horses have been relocated?"

She lifted her chin. "I've changed my mind."

He started. "You have?"

"Yes. I let the fear take over for a minute. No one is going to force me to run away from my sister's ranch. I'm staying until we've been able to find the horses good homes."

The emotion that washed over his face amused her. He was clearly nonplussed for some reason, this man who seemed perpetually in control. "Nice to hear the 'we.' I'll stick it out with you for as long as you need."

Her face warmed. Though he was every bit the soldier, from broad shoulders to wide stance, she could not help but see in him the seventeen-year-old hero who had rescued her mother's horse. "That is beyond kind. I want you to know how much I appreciate your help." She quickly added, "With the horses."

He gave her the glimmer of a smile.

She took a breath to clear her head and took off for the corral before her determination could wane. "We need to ride them. Cassie said in her journal the only way they'll get adopted is if we make them comfortable with a saddle."

"Good enough." Logan fell into step next to her. "Sheila called to check on you and she mentioned Bentley is at their place. I told her we'd meet him there."

"Let's ride over."

Logan hesitated. "We could take the truck."

She raised an eyebrow. "You don't like riding?"

"It's not my favorite thing. I'd rather be in a tank than on a horse. At least a tank only goes where you tell it to."

She laughed. "We can take the truck, if you feel that uncomfortable."

"No, no. Horseback is fine."

He approached the horses with enthusiasm and confidence she suspected he didn't feel. He did the work competently enough, and Isabel saddled Blue Boy while Logan did the same with a spotted horse named Striker.

She mounted Blue Boy carefully and, though he shook his head, he allowed her to gather up the reins. "I wasn't sure he'd let me for a minute there," she called to Logan as he mounted his horse.

"Maybe he knows you and Cassie were related."

The thought made her eyes fill. *I hope he doesn't know how I let her down.*

Logan cleared his throat. "I'm sorry. I forgot that Blue Boy was…"

"The horse that threw my sister." She reached down and patted the horse's neck. "If he throws me, then maybe I'll believe that's what happened to Cassie, but for now, I'm going to trust him. Cassie loved him."

Isabel followed Logan down a dirt trail that wound through a thick copse of spruce. Logan rode easily and Isabel would never have suspected he wasn't born in the saddle. The branches closed over them, bringing welcome shade and thick shadow that dappled them as they made their way along. She remembered the shock of seeing Autie sitting in the front room of Cassie's house, a gun perched on his lap as casually as if it had been a book.

You lack courage and commitment. You ran when you were sixteen and you will run again. What scared her the most was not that Autie seemed determined to drive her away, back to the grasp of Rawley; it was the fact that he knew her, deep down. He knew of her deepest sins.

How long had he been studying her? Soaking up the darkest of her memories and waiting to use them against her?

A branch snapped underfoot and she jerked in the saddle, causing Blue Boy to shake his mane. The trees grew thicker until their branches grazed the edges of the narrow path. She caught a glimpse of a lake in the distance, the eerie glimmer of water shrouded by trees. She imagined Autie hidden just out of sight, humming his strange tunes, tracking her as she moved.

I will be happy to make you disappear.

Disappear.

A branch caught the back of her shirt and she barely contained a scream.

Sweat trickled down her back and she felt the flicker of an insect buzz her head.

Autie's pale eyes seemed to be watching her from every shadow until she felt like screaming.

Instead she urged Blue Boy to close the gap between them and Logan's horse. He could not do anything if Autie's bullet ripped through the gloom and found her head. Nonetheless, Logan's nearness comforted her until they emerged from the woods at the entrance to the Trigg property.

A long driveway led to a sprawling ranch-style home. Well-tended fences marked a series of corrals and, beyond that, acres of grassland dotted with some of the loveliest horses Isabel had ever seen. The sheriff's car was parked near a detached building Isabel took to be a garage. An SUV was up on blocks in front, and an open toolbox lay nearby.

Logan and Isabel led the horses to an empty corral and let them loose to crop at the choicest grass they could find. Blue Boy edged Striker away from the greenest patch and set to work.

Isabel smiled. Her legs felt a bit wobbly from the ride and she had to laugh. "It's been a long time since I've ridden. You did pretty well for a guy who doesn't like horses."

"I didn't say I couldn't ride them. They just aren't my first choice of transportation."

She laughed, feeling an inexplicable happiness that momentarily drove thoughts of Autie out of her mind.

A shout came from the garage.

The sound of angry male voices poured out of the shaded opening. Isabel couldn't make out who was yelling, but when Logan took off in the direction of the ruckus, she followed.

Inside the small structure, it took her eyes a moment to adjust to the darkness before she made out the identities of the two men.

Officer Bentley stood with his hands on his hips, head slightly bowed.

John Trigg, flushed red and lips thin with rage, faced him.

"Take off, Bentley," he hissed. "Take yourself away from this place and don't ever come back. I won't be responsible for what happens if you do."

Isabel couldn't hear Bentley's murmured reply. She watched in horror as John Trigg exploded in rage. His fist shot out and smashed into Bentley's face.

EIGHT

Logan leaped into the fray as Bentley tried to scramble to his feet and John went after him again, knocking him to the ground. John shouted as he tried to get a hold around Bentley's neck.

Logan shoved John off.

He fell backward, giving Bentley time to make it to his feet. Blood streamed out of the officer's nose and down his chin, spattering the front of his khaki uniform. He tried to stop the flow with the back of his hand.

"Not going to solve anything this way," Bentley muttered.

Logan saw John about to launch another attack. With a resigned sigh, he grabbed the man and restrained him, planting him facedown with his hands behind his back. "John, you need to calm down."

John wriggled and swore but he could not free himself. Logan kept him pinned there while Isabel tried to help Bentley.

The officer shook her off. Without looking at John, he stalked from the garage, leaving a trail of blood droplets on the ground. Logan wondered why Bentley didn't arrest John on the spot.

Logan waited a moment and then released the pressure

slightly. "Keep yourself under control or we'll be doing this again."

John got to his feet and brushed the grit from his hands. "Stay out of it, Logan."

"If that means letting you kill the sheriff, I don't think so."

"Not your job to be the hero. You're a contractor now." His eyes glittered. "A working stiff, like the rest of us."

Logan felt the sting of those words. With an effort, he kept his voice level. "And this contractor isn't going to let you kill the sheriff either."

Carl came huffing into the garage, cheeks red from the effort. "Everybody okay? Bentley looks like he went five rounds with Muhammad Ali." His gaze wandered from Logan to John. "That your handiwork, son?"

John snorted, but didn't answer.

Carl's shoulders slumped. "We've been through this. What's done is done. You need to let it go."

"Can't."

"You got to."

John spat out the words. "Just because you did, doesn't mean I'm gonna." He stalked past his father and Isabel and left.

Carl smiled wanly and moved to Logan to shake his hand. "I assume you kept my son from taking a walk on the stupid side?"

Logan shrugged, catching the faintest whiff of alcohol on Trigg's breath. "Just broke up a brawl. What's going on here?" He'd always known John had a temper, since their days in high school, but the outburst still surprised him, especially since it involved Bentley.

Carl waved a hand. "Too ridiculous to go into. Come into

the house, both of you, and we'll try to show you some better hospitality than this."

Logan saw the puzzlement on Isabel's face as she joined them.

They found Sheila in the massive kitchen, handing Bentley a towel as he sat at the long pine table. There was no sign of John. She wrapped Isabel in a hug and then Logan. "I'm so glad you were here. That son of mine. What am I going to do with him? He's still a ten-year-old kid with a chip on his shoulder." She laughed, but Logan could see real pain in her eyes. He burned with curiosity to know the root of John's hostility toward Bentley, but could think of no polite way to dig for information.

Sheila insisted they sit down and slid glasses of iced tea in front of them. Carl was drinking something that Logan suspected was not tea.

Carl bobbed his chin at them. "Officer Bentley tells me you had another problem at the ranch."

Isabel shot an uneasy look at Logan. He nodded encouragingly at her.

She told them about Autie's visit.

Sheila pressed a hand to her mouth. "In the house? You must have been terrified."

He saw Isabel swallow hard. "I'm not going to let him scare me away."

Carl huffed. "Good for you. Show that lunatic who is in control."

Sheila's eyes were still round with horror. "You can't mean you're going to stay out there all alone? With some crazy person after you? That's just nuts." She appealed to the sheriff. "Tell her that's crazy."

His face remained expressionless under his purpling nose. "He might have meant to scare her and he's gone. Could be he's cleared out."

She slapped her hand on the table. "Well, I wouldn't bet the girl's safety on that." She turned to Isabel. "I think you should stay here with us, until the lawyers can arrange to have the property sold."

Logan drained the tea. "That might be a good idea. What do you think, Isabel?"

She shook her head. "I want to stay near the horses."

"You could tend them every day. John could ride over with you and be sure that crazy man isn't lurking around somewhere."

Logan spoke quickly. "I'll help with the horses. I'm going to finish clearing the ravine anyway, so I'll pull up my tent trailer and camp out at the ranch." He hadn't even given a thought to the matter before, but here came the plan, fresh from his lips. He tried for a tone of nonchalance, wondering what Isabel was thinking, but not daring to look at her.

Sheila's mouth opened in surprise. "I thought you'd sell those horses off at the first opportunity."

"That's the plan. They will be adopted out, but we've got to work with them and find homes that fit."

She laughed. "The tough pararescue hero really is a softy, isn't he?"

Logan felt the heat rise to his cheeks. "It's what Cassie wanted."

She nodded. "Isabel, I want you to know the money Cassie left for us is going to be used to plan her memorial, and whatever is left over goes back to providing for the horses."

Isabel's smile was joyful as Sheila took her hands. "There's no need for you to do that," Isabel said. "She wanted you to have the money."

"Carl and I insist."

Carl nodded. "Put your sister to rest properly." His eyes shone with tears.

Isabel blinked. "Thank you."

Sheila stood and fetched the pitcher to refill their glasses. "Of course. We wouldn't hear of anything else."

Isabel cleared her throat. "And I want to do the Moonlight Ride."

Logan's surprise was mirrored in the other faces at the table.

"No one would blame you for pulling out," Carl said.

Isabel raised her chin. "Cassie wanted the horses to participate, to be seen. It might help them find homes, and it's an important fund-raiser for a group she felt passionate about."

Logan was mesmerized by the determination that shone from her dark eyes, the courage written in the tilt of her head, the strength of her words. He wished he had a gift for sketching, so he could capture the expression on her face that made his heart beat faster.

After they'd returned the horses to the ranch and given them free rein in the pasture, Isabel found herself seated next to Logan in the front seat of his truck. As he drove down the steep mountain road toward his condo, he drummed his fingers on the steering wheel. "I should have talked to you about my plan." He shot a quick look at her. "To camp out in my tent trailer at your place."

She pulled the hair from her face and secured it against the wind rushing in the open window. "It's a lot to ask."

"You didn't ask. I lined out the mission all by myself." He gave her a rueful smile. "Leftover from my previous job."

"What branch of the service?"

"Pararescue. Air Force folks who go in and pull people out of the fire. Sort of a mobile ambulance, if you will."

"Sounds dangerous."

"It is," he grunted. "It was."

She saw emptiness and longing written in his eyes. "You miss it."

"Like an arm or leg. I busted up my ankle on a mission that went bad. My only hope now is to get hired on as an instructor."

"Would that satisfy you?"

He sighed. "I would sweep floors and empty trash cans, if that's what they needed."

She looked at his strong profile, the way he leaned forward a bit when he talked about his work. "Well, it's okay by me if your new mission is sleeping in your tent trailer at the ranch, but it doesn't sound very comfortable."

He laughed. "Trust me, I've slept in worse conditions. Much worse. But why didn't you take the Triggs up on their offer to stay?"

Isabel mulled it over. Why hadn't she? It was some indefinable feeling about John Trigg that had risen in her gut even before they had come upon him punching the sheriff. "I'm not sure. Maybe the fighting. What does John Trigg have against Bentley?"

"I don't know. I would have said nothing if I hadn't seen them going at it today."

But it had been one-sided, she thought. Bentley hadn't thrown any punches in return or arrested John, and what had John said to his father about letting things go?

"Just because you did, doesn't mean I'm gonna."

Whatever it was, the three of them were involved in something painful.

They arrived at Logan's condo and Isabel thought the place matched his personality; orderly, precise, neat. She peered at the photos of him with his buddies. Cassie's unmailed letter hinted that he'd had a wife, but there was no evidence of much feminine influence.

Her attention was arrested by a precisely folded flag.

Logan returned from hitching up the tent trailer and packing a small duffel bag. "A buddy of mine didn't make it. He had no family. That's why I have the flag."

She wanted to touch him then, to bring him into her arms and ease away the heavy grief in his words. Her own desire startled her. She'd only loved two men in her life and both her father and Rawley hurt her to the core. Stepping away, she put her hands in her pockets. A memory poked at her.

"Autie sang something about a flag."

The phone rang and he gestured for her to sit on the couch. "Hey, Bill. I'm putting you on speakerphone. Isabel Ling, Cassie's sister, is here with me."

Bill's voice was low and soft as he greeted them.

Logan leaned forward. "What do you have for us? The guy goes by the name of Autie and he's paid Isabel another visit."

"Something about this case is eating at me, but I couldn't find any matches, Logan. I contacted some old-timers from the region and talked them up a little, but they need more to go on. Anything you can provide?"

Isabel related some of the conversation she'd had with Autie, giving Bill details about the clothes and his gun. "And he knows…many of the details of my life." She did not want to talk about her past, especially not in front of Logan, but Bill was caught on a detail.

"Slouch hat and boots. Long hair. What did he call you?"

"I'm sorry?"

"Miss Ling? Isabel? What did he call you?"

"Ma'am." Her eyes drifted back to the flag. "I was just remembering he sang an odd song the day he pushed me in the ravine, and again at the cemetery. I can't recall all of it, but it was something about the flag and a drummer boy."

Bill's tone was grim. *"And the lovely old flag?"*

"Yes, that's it. How did you know?"

There was a pause. "Because I know who your bad guy is, or more accurately, I know who his father is."

Logan stood. "Tell us."

"I didn't figure it out until you told me about the song. That's an old Civil War tune. Put that together with the hat, long hair, his antiquated speech patterns."

Isabel frowned. "I don't understand. Do you know Autie? Who is he?"

"Autie was the nickname of George Custer, the famous U.S. cavalry commander. Your Autie is actually Oscar Birch. I knew Autie's father. I put him in prison last year, actually."

A muscle in Logan's jaw twitched. "So Autie's father is the one—"

Bill finished. "Who killed my partner."

Isabel gasped. "How awful!"

Bill's voice shook only once as he continued. "We were tracking Oscar Senior for months. The guy is a complete Civil War nut. He had shelves of books about Custer, everything ever written on the man. He collected weapons from the era and even dressed the part. He raised his son to be a fanatic as well. Social services went out a few times investigating Oscar as a potential wife beater, but she'd never say a word against him. Neither would the son, of course. Daddy is his hero. We always suspected Autie helped his father hide from us for such a long time, but we could never prove it. Autie was never charged with anything. He's got no criminal record."

Logan began to pace. "What can you tell us about him then?"

"Only a few things. He is an accomplished survivalist. He's also brilliant. His mother homeschooled him, from what I gather, and he has a photographic memory."

"He grew up around here?"

"In and around the Dakotas. He knows the area, Logan. We finally caught up to his father, holed up in a cave in the Black

Hills. Wouldn't have found him, except my partner Johnny was Lakota and used to camp in those hills. Oscar prepared an ambush and Johnny was killed by an explosive."

Isabel heard the tremor of emotion in Bill's voice again. What had it been like for Bill to track Autie's father to the place where his partner would be murdered?

Logan appeared deep in thought.

Bill cut in again. "I am going to forward my files to your head of police. It might not hurt to have Cassie's death report looked at again. I have a feeling what's happening now is somehow connected. Who's in charge there?"

"Guy named Bentley."

"He worth his badge?"

Isabel thought Logan hesitated before he answered. "Far as I know."

"I'm going to try to get clear of some things here and I'll come."

Logan smiled. "I was hoping you'd say that. Tank will be happy to see you."

"He's glad to see anyone who isn't a squirrel." Bill laughed and then his tone sobered. "Be careful, both of you. The Birch men are crazy, but smart, too. They don't make mistakes often."

Isabel marshaled her fear into words. "Bill, before you go, can I ask you something?"

"Sure."

"Why were you looking for Oscar Senior? What crime did he commit?" She locked eyes with Logan as Bill's answer filled the room.

"He murdered his wife, Autie's mother."

NINE

Logan watched the reaction on Isabel's face. He knew Cloudman's story only from the scant details he and some other acquaintances in law enforcement had provided. Bill and his partner, with appropriate backup, had arrived at the spot where they'd expected to apprehend Oscar Senior. Oscar was gone, but he'd rigged an explosive charge that had detonated the moment Cloudman's partner stepped on the trigger wire.

Bill had refused to talk more about it, quit his position as a Tribal Ranger and left his life behind. Logan knew it was not just the loss of his friend, but Bill's own sense of failure and defeat that drove him. If he'd only been there first. If he'd just seen the tripwire. If only, if only.

Logan knew that feeling. He'd lost people, soldiers and civilians, when he hadn't been quick enough, or smart enough, to second-guess the enemy. He never forgot those faces, the eyes that looked into his with desperation, or resignation, as the life leaked out of them, and all he could do was hold onto the victim's hand and silently apologize for not saving them.

Tell my wife I love her.
Did my guys make it out?
Make sure my kid knows I did my job.

Their last messages played in his mind, clear as the day he'd heard them.

He jerked himself away from the pain. Isabel was standing next to him, her hand on his arm. "Are you okay?"

"I should be asking you that. What do you think about Bill's information?"

"At least I know who Autie is. I feel more strongly than ever he had something to do with Cassie's accident." She looked thoughtful. "Do you know why Oscar killed his wife?"

"I'm not sure anyone knows that besides maybe Autie. I'll ask Bill when he calls back. Still want to stay at the ranch? It's not too late to change your mind. There's a hotel in town or the Triggs' place."

She smiled. "I'm stubborn, you see, and I've always done things the hard way."

"Me, too." He led her to the truck. The long rays of late afternoon sun were giving way to a spectacular sunset behind the black cliffs. As they drove back, his curiosity got the better of him. "I was surprised when I first heard Cassie had a sister. She spoke about her mother often, but I don't remember hearing about you."

Isabel looked out the window. "I ran away when I was sixteen. It hurt my sister and we didn't talk at all until I got up the courage to send her a letter a few months ago."

"Why did you run away?" For a moment, he thought she wasn't going to answer until she let out a sigh.

"My father was an alcoholic. When his machine shop failed, he fell apart. He directed his anger at my mother, never physically, but belittled her and criticized everything she did. I think he loved her deep down and when her lupus became life threatening he couldn't take it. He was scared, I think, but I didn't realize it at the time."

Logan nodded, afraid to talk in case he made her close up.

"Basically, he lived at the bar, and my sister and I cared for

Mom." A dreamy smile came over her face. "I used to draw pictures and tape them all over her bedroom walls. There wasn't a square inch of that room that wasn't wallpapered in my sketches. Anyway, when she died, I started to skip school, sneak out to go sit at her grave or ride her horse. When the principal called my dad one day, he took all my sketchbooks and drawings and burned them in the yard. I freaked out, yelled at him. I wanted to hurt him for hurting me. He slapped my face so hard I think sometimes I can still feel it. I turned and walked away and never came back until now."

Logan was shocked at the intensity of what she'd experienced and shocked that it awakened such a surge of emotion inside him. He hated the thought of her artwork being put to the match and of the shame that kept her from her sister all those years. "That's a lot to deal with."

"I tried to call Cassie a few times, years later, but they'd moved out of the home I grew up in and I..." She laced her fingers together. "I made some bad choices and fell into a life that turned me into someone else. Someone Cassie wouldn't recognize."

He thought about his ex-wife, Nancy. She'd turned into someone else, the kind of person who would sleep with another man while he was deployed. He felt the anger start to kindle until a strange notion startled him. Had he ever shared enough with Nancy to really know her in the first place? He'd been gone so much and, when he was there, he wanted the easy, conflict-free dynamic. Maybe he hadn't really wanted to see what was going wrong. He saw the quiver in Isabel's lip. He put a hand over hers and squeezed the delicate fingers. "Those are the kind of choices that can follow you forever, if you let them."

She looked at him, her hand tightening in his. "Have you made choices like that?"

There was a deep yearning in her voice.

His uncle's voice rumbled through his memory. "Keep God in your head, Logan. Remember, whatever you ask for in prayer, believe that you have received it and it will be yours." He'd done plenty of praying, but since Nancy's betrayal and his injury, his prayers focused around only one thing: getting back into pararescue. He recalled the rest of Mark 11:24.

"And when you stand praying, if you hold anything against anyone, forgive him, so that your Father in heaven may forgive you of your sins."

He knew for a fact God had pulled him out of the line of fire on multiple occasions, and God would hear his prayers now and return him to pararescue. But was that the only thing he was supposed to be praying for? What about forgiveness for his part in a failed marriage? And what about the courage to forgive the woman who had cheated on him? He'd never so much as spent a moment praying for those things.

He wanted to tell Isabel, to unburden himself about the mess he'd made of it all, but it was too much. Mistakes couldn't be unmade and the only thing that mattered was the next mission.

Finish Cassie's job. Find homes for the horses. Rejoin the military.

His future in pararescue was the only possible scenario.

Isabel was still looking at him. Had he made choices that turned him away from who he was meant to be? He let go of her hand. "Too many to count."

Isabel kept Tank out of the way as Logan put up the tent trailer under the shelter of some trees near the house. She still felt guilty that he would go to the trouble, but relief won out. As much as she wanted to care for Cassie's horses, the thought of being at Mountain Cloud alone, with Autie waiting in the shadows, was intolerable.

How would she ever be able to thank Logan?

By getting those horses adopted out as quickly as possible and freeing him from his responsibility. The horses were an obligation, and somehow she had become one, too. The least she could do was fix the man some dinner.

She put a hand on the front door to open it when Logan's shout stopped her.

"Don't, Isabel."

Heart pounding, hand still touching the knob, she froze.

He gestured for her and she walked to him, nerves prickling.

"Autie's struck again." He pointed to a cable on the backhoe where it still sat on top of the trailer. It had been neatly sliced. "Hydraulic fluid is still leaking out, so it was done recently. He could still be here."

Isabel had the urge to scream but she forced herself to remain calm. "Wouldn't Tank know if Autie was hiding on the ranch?"

Logan looked grim. "Tank is a great dog, but he's a little lacking in some areas. I want you to stay here. I'm going to check the house and barn. Do you have your phone?"

She nodded.

"Call the police and tell them what's up."

Thinking she should put the police on speed dial, she watched Logan gingerly enter the house, Tank at his heels. She held her breath as he crept across the threshold, head low, body tense. She relayed the information to the dispatcher at the police station who could track Bentley down.

Logan returned and pointed to the barn. While he was inside, there was a rush of noise from the pasture. Isabel prepared to take off running into the barn to warn Logan of Autie's return, when John Trigg appeared, Cassie's horses following him into the corral. He ducked his head at her as he rode past on his own mount.

"Thought you'd need help getting the horses bedded down for the night."

She let out a sigh of relief. "Logan is checking the barn. There's been more trouble."

He fastened the gate behind the horses and tied his own outside. "Trouble seems to follow you."

She ignored his barb. "I didn't expect to see you here tonight."

He shrugged. "Cassie would want me to take care of the horses."

Isabel heard something in the way he said her sister's name, a tiny shade of longing. Had he been in love with Cassie like Sheila suggested? She didn't have time to consider, as Logan emerged from the barn and headed for the smaller wood-sided structure nearby.

"What's in there?" she asked John.

"Tools, saddles and such. Mostly everything that didn't fit in the barn or garage." John passed a hand over his furrowed brow, baked brown from the South Dakota sun.

A question popped into Isabel's mind. "John, were you surprised at how my sister died?"

He almost jumped. "Surprised?"

"You knew her well. She was an expert rider. Did it seem strange to you that she took Blue Boy out at night and got thrown?"

He stared at her. "Plenty of things seem strange to me in this place, Isabel, especially the women who live here. I don't pretend to understand the choices they make."

She wondered at the bitterness in his tone. Was he talking about Cassie? Or someone else? Sheila's words came back to her.

John was never much with people, and he's been gun-shy since his last girlfriend moved away without leaving a forwarding address. She wanted to press further. "Do you think…?"

"I got no idea why your sister would have gone out riding at night. Maybe to prepare Blue Boy for the Moonlight Ride."

"Maybe, but Blue Boy doesn't startle easily. I just can't see him throwing her."

"As I said, plenty of strange things around here, Isabel. You're just going to make yourself crazy worrying about it. Better to let it go."

He was probably right, but she knew she could not, especially with Autie tracking her like a wounded animal. She had the unshakable feeling that Autie knew something about Cassie's death, and she was beginning to wonder if John did, too. A truck engine sounded in the gloom, starting its climb up the mountain. "That's probably Officer Bentley."

Trigg's eyes narrowed. "The horses are taken care of for now. I'll be back tomorrow sometime."

She felt the strong urge to pry more information from him. "Why don't you stay, John? Sooner or later I'm going to try to make some dinner. It's the least I can do for all your help with this place."

He looked at the ground. "I'd have done anything for your sister. Time for me to go." He unhitched the horse and swung easily into the saddle, urging the mare into a trot as he disappeared over the hill.

The darkness was almost complete. It closed around her, and Isabel wished Logan would return. She couldn't imagine what was taking him so long.

Her phone rang. She figured it was Bentley telling her he was on his way up the mountain.

The voice was sweet and slow. "Hello, ma'am."

Her fingers clenched around the phone, her stomach constricting painfully. "Autie. Are you calling to try to scare me some more?"

He laughed. "Am I scaring you, ma'am?"

She took a deep breath. "No. Should I be scared? Are you a murderer like your father?"

The tone changed abruptly. Autie's words were thick with rage. "Aren't you the clever girl? Trying to beat me at my own game? You know nothing about my father."

"I know he killed a Tribal Ranger." She hesitated a moment before she added, "And your mother."

Autie's voice hissed through the line. "That is the price for abandonment. It's time for you to go home, Isabel. Go back to your husband and your sad life in Southern California. While I have enjoyed our little skirmish, it's time for it to draw to a conclusion. Do you understand me?"

She had to steady the phone in her trembling hand. A cool breeze toyed with her hair, and the trees seemed to creep toward her through the darkness. She squeezed her bare arms to her body. "Leave me alone."

He laughed, the jovial tone back in place. "Why, Isabel. You sound a bit snappish. Perhaps you should go inside and put on a sweater. You look cold."

The line went dead as she dropped the phone and ran, blundering blindly through the darkness until someone caught her arm.

She screamed.

Logan stared into her face. "What is it? What's wrong?"

She panted. "A phone call… Autie. He can see me from wherever he called."

Logan looked around and marshaled her toward the house just as Officer Bentley's car appeared at the foot of the driveway. He eased out of the car, his nose swollen and purple. Logan filled him in. In a matter of minutes, he'd freed his gun from the holster and begun a search of the area behind the cabin. Logan went with Isabel into the house, sticking close as she wrapped herself in Cassie's tattered sweater with the button missing.

He was watching. Still watching. The thought nearly drove her mad. She looked at Logan, desperate to move her mind away from Autie. "What did you find in the shed?"

He shook his head. "Not sure."

She stared at him. "What are you not telling me?"

He looked out the window. "We can talk about it later, after I run it by Bentley."

Isabel felt her jaw tighten. "Why won't you tell me now?"

Logan looked startled at her question. "No need to upset you until I check it out thoroughly."

"I'm not a child."

"I know."

"If I can handle a stalker without going to pieces, you can tell me about the shed."

He looked dubious. "It's not…"

"Don't patronize me."

His green eyes flashed. "I'm trying to do what's right for you."

"You don't get to decide that."

He fisted his hands on his narrow hips. "Maybe you should trust me here."

"Tell me." The firmness in her own words surprised her. She felt anything but certain inside. All she knew was she had to take control of something or she'd be lost again.

Logan was saved from having to answer when Bentley returned, panting slightly. "No sign of him. I'm sure he's holing up somewhere nearby, but he's good at covering his tracks. I'm going to call in a reserve deputy and have him stick around here tonight. We'll do a more thorough search in the morning."

Logan nodded to Bentley. "I need to show you something

in the shed." As he started toward the door, Isabel followed. He gave her a frustrated glance but did not try to stop her. Just outside, he told Tank to sit and they entered the small space, filled with the scent of old leather and musty earth. The metal shelves were overflowing with clippers, bales of wire and boxes of various size nails. Against one wall was a row of pegs with bridles and an old saddle that looked as though it hadn't seen the light of day in a long time.

Logan knelt in the corner and took a penlight from his back pocket. "Here." He trained the beam into the darkness.

Bentley blocked her view as he knelt. After a moment, he rose and exchanged a look with Logan.

Isabel could wait no more. She shouldered past Bentley and peered into the shadows. At first she thought there was nothing at all but a lonely spider scrabbling to escape the light. When her vision adjusted she understood why Logan hadn't wanted her to come into the shed.

A dark spot on the floor, a bloodstain that spoke of long-ago violence.

And there, trapped behind a splinter of wood, were several long strands of dark hair.

She knew who they belonged to.

It was her sister's hair.

TEN

The room spun, walls whirling into confusion. She didn't know how she got out of the shed. Her stumbling feet and Logan's firm arm around her shoulders led her back to the cabin.

"Bentley's going to take photographs and secure the scene. It's all over for now."

She looked at him in horror. "It's just beginning. My sister was killed in that shed. Murdered, probably by the same man who is out there watching me."

He sat next to her. "We don't know that. The police will investigate more seriously now, but you had no connection with your sister since you were sixteen. What would be Autie's motive to kill either one of you?"

"I don't know. I thought Rawley was behind it, punishing me by taking away anything that matters." She bit her lip against a wave of panic.

Logan's voice was low and soothing. "How much did Rawley know about Cassie?"

"Everything. I thought he was a good man, one that I would be with forever. I thought he understood me, but that was part of his game. He listened, sympathized and made people think he was on their side. It was only later, much later, that I saw him clearly." She jerked to her feet and began to pace. "If

Rawley arranged to have Cassie killed…then I am the reason my sister died."

Logan went to her and grabbed hold of her shoulders. "Do not go there. You did not kill anyone, and whoever is to blame will be caught and punished. Don't do that to yourself, Isabel."

She tried to hold steady, but her body began to tremble. He pulled her close, stroking her hair and pressing his face to her cheek. She clung to him as if he was holding her afloat in an angry ocean. The words stuttered out, broken and painful. "I've prayed and prayed, to trust the right person, to be forgiven for my stupid mistakes. I've prayed…" Her words were choked off by sobs.

"Then you've done the most important thing." He caught her tear on his outstretched finger. "You've appealed to the Commander in Chief, so to speak. He knows the truth and He'll help us find it."

Her body tingled at his touch. When he lowered his face to brush his lips to hers, she felt a gentle warmth seep into her. She allowed herself to be guided to the kitchen table and Logan rummaged through the cupboard for a can of soup and crackers. Tank wandered in and sat down on her feet. She welcomed the solid weight, anchoring her back in the present, pulling her from the sins of the past.

She was in a dream, a horrible dream, and she wondered when God would pull her out of it. "All the time, I knew something was wrong about the way Cassie died." She looked at Logan. "Do you think Autie's been trying to scare me off before the murder came to light?"

"Why would he?"

"Because he was hired to."

Logan frowned. "Could be, but it's possible this has nothing to do with Rawley. In any case, the murder is not going to be a secret any longer. If Autie was hired to cover it up, or if he killed Cassie himself, it's all out there now."

"You think Autie will take off?"

"Do you?"

She felt a glimmer of hope but it quickly died. "I wouldn't count on it."

"Probably the best thing."

Bentley knocked and shuffled in. "Got the shed taped off. Evidence guy is on his way. We'll do a full search of the property in the morning with as many people as I can borrow from county. If Autie's holing up nearby, we'll find him."

Logan nodded. "And what about the…evidence in the shed?"

"I've phoned the county coroner and arranged to have him go over Cassie's file, inch by inch." He cleared his throat. "If necessary, we should do an autopsy. Will you agree to it?"

Isabel cringed. The thought of exhuming her sister's body made her skin go clammy. She'd failed her sister by allowing the burial when she'd known something wasn't right. The only thing left was to see that Cassie received the justice she deserved.

"I will agree to anything that will uncover who killed her."

"And possibly who hired Autie to do it," Logan added.

Bentley's eyes narrowed. "What takes you to that conclusion?"

"Just being thorough, thinking it through."

Bentley folded his arms. "I am thorough, Logan. That's my job, and I'll look into all the possibilities."

"That means interviewing John Trigg again?"

Isabel caught the look that washed over Bentley's face before he controlled it. Reluctance? Resignation? Guilt? She couldn't decide, but Logan's comment brought up an idea she hadn't considered before. In the face of the terror surrounding

Autie Birch, she hadn't stopped to realize that the person who spent the most time with Cassie, and most likely was deeply in love with her, was John Trigg.

Would he hurt Cassie? A man who loved her and shared her dreams? She didn't want to believe it of him, but the days of blind trust were gone.

People hurt their loved ones all the time, Isabel.

Sometimes, they even killed them.

The search team consisted of Bentley and three other officers, two borrowed from county. Logan watched them go, wishing he could be in on the action. Instead he contented himself tending the horses until Isabel opened the door and invited him to come in for breakfast. He felt a surge of relief to see her standing there, small frame silhouetted against the morning sun. He'd only slept fitfully, part of him listening for sounds of Autie in the dark.

Isabel looked as though she'd slept about as well as he had. Her hair was pulled into a long braid, face freshly washed, but the circles under her eyes marked a sleepless night. She put a plate of scrambled eggs and toast on the table for him, followed by mugs of instant coffee.

"Hard night?"

She settled onto the chair with a sigh. "Uh-huh. How about you? Was it comfortable in the trailer?"

"Sure. Tank slept like a log, anyway."

She laughed. "No word from the search team?"

"No. Not yet. It's a slow process and they've got a lot of ground to cover."

Sheila Trigg arrived in the doorway, carrying a plate of muffins, her face alarmed. "What in the world has happened now?"

Isabel invited her to come in and join them at the table.

"Logan found evidence that might prove Cassie was murdered."

"Murdered? I thought it was an accident. She was thrown by a horse."

"I think my sister was murdered, and whoever did it tried to cover it up and make it look like an accident."

"It's too horrible for words." Sheila sank into the chair. "Never in a million years would I have thought it. I'm so sorry, honey. It must be awful for you."

Logan caught the look in Isabel's eyes, the one that showed she was very close to breaking down. "It's best to get everything out in the open. So what brings you by, Sheila?"

She raised an eyebrow. "Well, since you refused my request to work on our fence project, I have to come over here to see you. Actually, the Moonlight Ride coordination meeting is this morning and I'm on my way into town." She nodded to Isabel. "I know it's not a good time, but if you really mean to go through with it, you should be there."

Isabel straightened. "I don't seem to be doing much good around here. Could I go along with you?"

"Of course. And what about you, Logan? Coming, or are you staying here and playing with your tractor?"

"It's a backhoe. I'll come to the meeting, too, since I'm helping out with this event." He thought he saw relief wash over Isabel's face. It pleased him. "Let's go."

A half hour later they were part of a crowd of people, milling around a sun-baked field on the edge of town. Tables were set up to deliver assignments to participants and people of all ages came and went on foot and horseback. Isabel found herself welcoming the noise after the eerie quiet of Mountain Cloud Ranch. There was safety in being swallowed up by this moving tide of people, knowing that Logan was nearby.

It was odd that he was continually present in her mind.

Since she'd heard Cassie's revelation that he was the young man who had rescued her mother years before, she couldn't shake the feeling that he'd been twined around her thoughts all that time. Though he was not the gangly teen standing in the rain, he looked at her with the familiar intensity in those green eyes that awakened a strange feeling inside.

Sheila pulled at her arm and pointed to a table. "Go there to find out how many guests you will be escorting on the ride."

She dutifully joined the end of the line, next to a pair of women deep in conversation.

John Trigg walked by, leading two unsaddled horses. He bobbed his head at the ladies and Isabel as he passed.

One of the women giggled and murmured to her friend. "He'd make a good catch. Daddy's going to be a senator soon."

The darker-haired woman snorted. "He's not exactly a lady's man. First Nora skipped town to get away, and the second one at the ranch up and died on him."

Isabel jerked, realizing the "second one" was her sister. Sheila hurried over and Isabel discerned she must have been close enough to overhear the gossip. As she bore down on them, the women hurriedly moved away.

Sheila sighed as she watched them go. "Don't pay them any mind, honey. This place is such a ridiculously small town in some ways."

Isabel decided to go for broke. "Who was Nora?"

Sheila shook her head. "A local girl. John had it bad for her. They dated for months until one day she packed up and left town without a word. It broke his heart." She gazed at the passing people. "That's the problem with having kids. You live through your own heartbreaks and then you have to live through theirs, only you can't do a thing about it."

There was such sadness in her face that Isabel reached out and squeezed her arm. "I'm sorry."

Sheila rolled her eyes. "I'm just in a funk. Must be this business about your sister." She waved at someone. "I've got to go meet Carl. We're doing a little dedication speech to get this event started." She gave Isabel a quick hug. "I really am glad you decided to participate. See you soon."

Isabel was surprised to see Dr. Lunardi manning the table when she got to the front of the line. He squinted in recognition, and then his lips narrowed. "Ms. Ling. I didn't know you were joining in."

"I'm making good on my sister's commitment."

"How nice." His tone was cold. "I heard from the sheriff this morning that your sister's case is being reopened. I have to say I resent the implication that I didn't do a proper examination to determine cause of death."

"No one implied that. Different facts have come to light."

He grimaced. "I've been the doctor on call in this town for fifteen years and now my reputation is being questioned."

"I'm sorry you feel that way, doctor."

"I don't think you're sorry at all." He shoved a manila envelope at her. "You are assigned to carry two guests. They've expressed an interest in adopting some horses, so we've got to make it a good experience for them. Can you supply rider-worthy horses for the event?"

Could she? She'd had so little time with them. But Cassie must have thought they could be trusted to carry people. With a smile she reached for the envelope. "Of course. I assume all the details are in here?"

"Yes. Next in line, please."

She turned away, scanning the crowd for Logan. They had a lot to talk about.

* * *

Logan was on his way back to meet Isabel in the field, new hydraulic line in a coil under his arm and a bag of bagels in the other. Tank darted into the tree line after some critter that Logan couldn't see. He was about to call him back, when his phone rang. He juggled things around and answered on the third ring.

"Slowing down, Price?"

Logan snapped to attention. "Sir, no, sir."

The senior staff sergeant laughed. "Good. Wouldn't want to put you through extended day training again."

Logan remembered the grueling nineteen-hour session. Sleep deprived and exhausted, struggling to pull on a wet suit, swimming endlessly before returning for a medical terminology class. It was the worst experience of his life.

And he'd do it again in a heartbeat.

At the moment, his heart was pounding so hard he thought he'd crack a rib.

"Been thinking about you, Price. How's the ankle?"

"In good shape, sir."

"Keeping up on the rehab?"

"Sir, yes, sir."

"I've got your application for trainer on my desk. We're considering."

Logan held his breath.

"I wanted to tell you straight out. It's not the same, son. Just so you know. A trainer is a different animal than being on a team. Trainers give soldiers the skills and then watch them go. You can't regain what you lost, if that's what you're after. Trainers are trainers, not squad brothers. Would you be okay with that, son?"

He swallowed. Apart from the excitement, the heart-stopping exhilaration of literally plucking a soldier from certain death, he'd relished being one of seven, a tight-knit family that knew everything, shared everything and bore everything together. Brothers. His team was the only place where his vulnerabilities didn't make him weak, but connected him to a group that made him strong, wove them all into an invincible unit.

Invincible.

He'd believed it, until his ankle had shattered like a piece of brittle glass.

And the team moved on.

Without him.

"Price? I asked you a question."

"Sir, yes, sir. I would be proud to serve pararescue in any capacity available."

"All right. We'll be in touch soon."

He stood holding the phone for a moment, trying to sort through the emotions. The one that floated to the top was hope. The sergeant wouldn't have called unless they were seriously considering his application. He let the feeling swirl around inside before he checked it.

One thing at a time. You've got a bunch of horses to find homes for and a ravine to clear. Tank galloped up in response to his whistle and, with a renewed sense of urgency, Logan caught up with Isabel as she stood thumbing through a set of papers.

She looked up and gave him a worried smile that set his heart thumping again. "Logan, do we have two horses trustworthy enough to carry people on the Moonlight Ride?"

"Not sure. Did you already commit?"

A flush crept into her cheeks. "Well, I sort of told them we did."

He laughed. "You'd have made a great pararescueman. Let's go back to Mountain Cloud and find out if we can deliver on your promise."

ELEVEN

Isabel thought Blue Boy looked peeved that he was not saddled for a ride like his compatriots, Striker and Echo. The horses patiently endured Isabel's efforts to saddle them and allowed themselves to be led out of the corral. Tank fired off a couple of cautious barks that elicited no response from the animals as they set off.

"Do you have a route in mind, Logan?"

He pointed to a path that sloped down, away from Cassie's property. "The search team is working north of here so I figured we'd take the horses in the opposite direction. They've already done a cursory search of that area so it's safe. There's a lake down there and the terrain is somewhat uneven, so we can see how well they do."

She shivered. "Do you think Autie's still around?"

"With all the commotion and police action, I don't think so, but if we see any sign of his presence we'll turn around and alert the cops."

She mounted Echo and followed Logan's horse down the trail.

As they headed through the trees, she breathed deeply of the air filled with the smell of spruce and the faintest scent of horse. The sun on her cheeks felt as though it could burn away the worry in her stomach, the terror about Autie, the strange facts about her sister's suspicious death. In that one moment, she felt the unfamiliar stirring of contentedness, following Logan's sturdy form into the South Dakota countryside.

He must have felt her watching because he turned and caught her eye. "Okay?"

She smiled. "Yes. I've got no reason to be okay, but for the moment, I can understand why Cassie loved this part of the world."

He raised an eyebrow. "You know, I've spent most of the last ten years living here without really considering it home."

"How so?"

He leaned back in the saddle and plucked a branch from a shrub as they passed. "It was just sort of a landing spot before the next mission. I guess I didn't really allow it to become home for me."

She wondered what Logan's ex-wife thought about it, but she didn't have the courage to ask. He answered it for her.

"Nancy talked about moving to New York, but I could never stomach the idea. Maybe I should have realized at that point how things were going between us."

"That's hard to see sometimes."

"I didn't want to see it. If I really took the time to look, I could have caught the signs that she was spending time with another man. My focus was elsewhere." He threw down the stick. "The downside of a one-track mind, I guess."

"Betrayal hurts, no matter what the circumstances."

"You got that right."

She wished she was close enough to take his hand and tell him about her own choices; the ones that had seemed so right at the time, the ones that had come back to ensnare her later.

Tank jerked and let out a loud bark before tearing off into the shrubbery. Logan whistled for him, but the dog didn't return. "He's probably after a squirrel. When he loses it, he'll come back."

The temperature rose steadily. They stopped for a quick snack of sandwiches and cold water and then continued down to the lake. Logan called for Tank several more times, but there was no sign of the dog.

The ground was dry, littered with brittle leaves that crackled under the weight of the horses as they picked their way down to the water. Logan had grown silent, wary. Isabel tried to follow his gaze as he stared intently into the trees.

"What do you hear?"

"Nothing. That's what worries me. No birds. No Tank. Too quiet."

The only sound was the wind rattling the dead leaves. Even the horses seemed to be listening. Fear rippled down her spine.

Logan's voice was intense when he spoke. "Isabel, ride back to the ranch."

"Now? What about you?"

"I'm going to check just over that rise and then I'll follow you." He tied the horse to a tree and went to the saddlebag.

She gasped when he removed a gun and loaded it. "Let's go back together."

He shook his head, eyes still trained on the place where the path disappeared at the top of a small slope. "I need to check it out, in case Tank is down there."

"You said Tank would find you."

"He should have come back by now. Something's wrong. Go back, Isabel. Quickly."

She reluctantly mounted Echo and urged him back down the path they had taken. She didn't want to leave Logan. Her senses screamed that he would not be safe, but she could tell from his tone, the set of his shoulders, he wasn't going anywhere until he'd made every effort to find Tank.

She watched him run to the tree line, moving swiftly in the ribbon of shade until he'd almost reached the top.

The two sounds came almost simultaneously.

A familiar bark.

And the explosion of a gunshot.

Logan hit the ground as soon as he saw the figure emerge on the path, holding firmly to Tank's collar. Though the dog jerked and snarled, Autie held him fast with one hand, a rifle in the other. Autie's shot whistled past and drilled itself into the trunk of a tree. Logan gripped his M9 pistol in front of him and rolled into the bushes for cover.

"How do you do, Captain Price? We have not had the pleasure of a meeting, but I believe I've got your dog here."

He didn't take time to consider how the guy knew his Air Force rank. "Let him go, Autie," he snapped, still under cover.

"Handsome animal. You should not leave the creature to run wild. Especially not around here. Never know what mischief he could get into."

"Don't hurt the dog," Logan called. He looked around to figure out a way to get closer to Autie without being seen. He rolled farther into the brush as quietly as he could manage.

Autie laughed. "A tough soldier like you has got a soft spot for the dog? Well, I do not blame you. I once had a cat that I was most attached to until the coyotes got her. But you are in an awkward spot, are you not? Maybe you should come on out in the open and we can discuss your situation."

"I'm not going to tell you again. Do not hurt that dog."

Autie sighed. "Generally I would not hurt any living creature unless it was strictly necessary, but this dog has complicated my mission, you see."

Tank let out a whine as Autie shook him. Logan gritted his teeth and decided on a plan. He tucked the pistol in his belt behind his back and belly-crawled closer to the wall of scrub that surrounded the trail on either side.

Through the screen of leaves he saw Autie look warily into the foliage. He raised the rifle and put it to Tank's head. The dog squirmed and thrashed, but Autie held on. "Captain Price, I respect your service to this fine country and I appreciate your love of dogs. I have no disagreement with you, per se, but I have a mission to complete and you and your dog are hampering my efforts."

Logan willed his breathing to stay steady. Autie was a survivalist and no doubt a crack shot. Logan would have time to squeeze off one round at most. No second chances. He continued to move another few feet toward a place where the ground rose slightly. A few feet below was the wide girth of a fallen tree. Easing his knees under him he mentally calculated the distance between his current location and the downed trunk that would provide cover.

A branch snapped under his knee. Autie fired into the scrub where Logan was hunkered down. The shot deafened him as it cut through the vegetation. He felt the whirr of hot metal as it winged by his head.

Autie's eyes narrowed. "Now then, Captain. I do hope you are not considering something that would put yourself at risk. Or the lovely Isabel. I am sure she is around here somewhere, is she not?"

He gritted his teeth, glad he'd sent her away.

Autie's head swiveled. "Ah. She must have ridden back. Keep the women and children safe? No matter. It will be an easy thing to catch up with her. And I will."

Logan flattened himself as much as he could, easing the pistol out from his belt, inch by painstaking inch.

"Nothing to say then? I am sorry you are not being cooperative, Captain. It is going to make it easier for me to kill you, after I dispatch your dog."

Logan was coiled to leap when a sharp crack made Autie turn, the sound of a twig snapping under the weight of a human foot. A rock sailed out of the foliage and grazed Autie's hat as it flew over. It was enough to make him loosen his grip on the dog. Tank tore out of his grasp and turned on the man, teeth bared and barking. Autie aimed the rifle again but before he could kill the dog, Logan leaped out of hiding, fired off a shot and tumbled behind the fallen log.

He looked out. Autie held his arm, blood trickling through the fingers, before he turned and ran into the brush. Tank started after him, but Logan called him off. Autie ran into the trees and vanished over the ridgeline.

The dog changed direction, hurtled behind the log and slobbered on Logan's face. He heaved a sigh of relief that Tank hadn't taken a round in the fracas. "Get off me, you crazy mutt. Why'd you let yourself get caught? What kind of dog are you?"

Isabel's voice startled them both. "I don't think he's much of a soldier."

Logan pulled her down next to him. "Didn't I tell you to get out of here?"

She raised an eyebrow. "I thought you knew I'm not the greatest at doing what I'm ordered to."

"Dumb thing to do, Isabel."

"I knew you would say that." She tried to look him over. "Are you hurt? Did he hit you anywhere?"

"No. I've been in tighter spots than that before." His emotions reached the flash point and he rounded on her. "What were you thinking? Autie could have killed you. Or I could have shot you." Friendly fire, a soldier's worst nightmare. A chill cut across his spine in spite of the heat.

"I didn't want him to hurt Tank. Or you."

"It was reckless and it could have gotten us all killed."

She looked at her lap and didn't answer.

A tremor in her lip took the rage right out of him. He put a hand around her shoulders and pulled her roughly to his side, continuing in a gentler tone. "Keep close until we make sure he isn't returning. You can do that much, can't you?"

She huddled into a ball in the circle of his arm and he felt her tremble.

"I didn't know where you were. I just saw Autie was about to shoot Tank so I threw a rock at him." She blinked hard.

Logan shook his head and sighed. "Nice shot."

"Not really, I was aiming for his stomach."

He would have laughed if the situation hadn't been so serious. He didn't allow himself to consider further what the alternative could have been. She was safe, that was the only acceptable result. He kept her close, her face hidden by a wave of hair that had escaped the braid. She sniffled and his remaining anger drained away.

With one finger, he pulled the fringe back. "I'm sorry I yelled. I'm used to giving orders and having them followed."

She shrugged and wiped her eyes with her sleeve. "Your dog doesn't seem to obey very well."

He grinned. "You got me there." He caressed her shoulder until her head relaxed against his chest. "Anyway, I'm sorry."

"You're forgiven."

No sound came from the woods but the click of an insect in the tree above them. He let the silence build for another five minutes. "I'm going to look around, see if he left anything behind. You don't want to hang out here and stay put, I suppose?"

She gave him a luscious smile that made him tingle. "No. I'm staying with you and Tank."

The dog gave her a sloppy lick to the cheek, which caused her to giggle.

"See if you can keep him out of trouble."

She mock saluted. "Yes, sir."

They kept low and headed down the path as it dropped away from the lake.

"Autie must have a camp set up somewhere. There should be the remnants of a fire. Some indication that he's been living out here. Must be subtle for the cops to have missed it. I see no vehicle tracks, so he's been getting around on foot."

They topped the rise and headed down into a wide hollow, crammed with trees and sprawling vegetation. Logan did a slow circle, hand shading his eyes from the harsh sun. A creek that fed into the lake meandered under the dense shrubbery.

Logan followed the path of the river until it disappeared into a steep ravine. "He's gonna need water, sooner or later. He'll want shelter from the wind and adequate visibility." He grabbed hold of a low pine branch and began to climb. Scrambling upward through layers of needles and avoiding the sap as best he could, he made his way up the tree until he had a view of the tangled forest below.

Isabel sat with Tank to keep him from whining and jumping at the tree trunk. Logan stared at the ground below. Nothing to see. No tent or backpack, no telltale sign of broken branches. He grunted in frustration and started to climb down when something caught his eye. It wasn't a flash of color or the glint of metal. There was a shape where it shouldn't have been, a straight line that didn't belong in the natural world.

He shimmied down as quickly as he dared and hustled into the brush.

Isabel followed. "What did you see?"

"I thought…" He looked again at the dark green and browns that would have concealed the thing completely, if the too-perfect outline hadn't given it away. Thrusting his arms into the brush, he shoved away the branches that had been cut to overlap the structure.

Isabel gasped. "I could have been standing right by it and I wouldn't have noticed."

"It's a hunting blind." The soft-sided rectangle was covered with canvas panels, sponged in the same colors as the surroundings. The walls were a good seven feet high, but so cleverly tucked into the scenery they might as well have been invisible.

The four small windows were precise cutouts in the walls, with no glass to catch the sunlight. They could be covered over with canvas flaps in an instant. "Autie is good," he muttered. "I'll give him that. These blinds go for upward of a thousand dollars, but he designed this one himself. It's better than anything I've ever seen."

A bird screamed out of the tree line, squawking.

His instincts filled him in before his brain could think it through.

They were not alone anymore.

Logan removed his weapon and pulled Isabel behind him.

She stumbled and fell against him, but he managed to keep her upright.

"What?" she breathed in his ear.

It was too late to take cover. Too late to retreat.

He eyed the trees grimly. Time to make a stand.

"Visitors."

TWELVE

Isabel thought it felt like an eternity, standing there in the stifling woods, listening to the sound of someone approaching. Her fingers gripped the back of Logan's shirt, and she could feel the tension radiating from his muscled back.

The sun burned down, bathing her in sweat, but she dared not raise a hand to wipe the salty trickle from her eyes.

A shout rang through the woods. "Police." Bentley and another officer pushed through the tree line, guns at the ready. "You guys okay? We heard shots."

She felt Logan exhale and he allowed Isabel to ease out from behind him. He stowed his pistol. "Autie took a few shots. I winged him in the shoulder. He headed east." Logan pointed to Autie's escape route.

The officer accompanying Bentley unclipped a radio and stepped away to talk.

Bentley came closer to examine the blind. "Nice setup. We totally missed it in the initial search."

Bentley's uniform was disheveled, his shirt showing dark sweat stains.

"Has anything come to light in my sister's case?" Isabel asked him.

He shook his head. "Coroner hasn't reported to me yet. Still looking over the files. We found nothing in our search

for Autie so far. I'm going to take a look in here and see if
he's left anything helpful."

He unzipped a flap that had been so cleverly constructed,
Isabel hadn't known it was there. Bentley stepped inside and
gestured for both Logan and Isabel to remain where they
were. They contented themselves by looking into the small
space, which contained a canvas blanket and a rucksack neatly
stacked in the corner. A Coleman lantern and a tattered copy
of *Custer's Last Stand* were the only other items.

Bentley used a pen to upend the rucksack, dumping a canteen, an apple and some silver pouches on the floor.

"MREs. Meals ready to eat," Logan said in her ear. She
wondered why he looked so worried when it seemed as though
they had finally gotten a break. Autie slipped up. He'd left
himself exposed. Now he was the one on the run and scared.
She couldn't suppress a surge of satisfaction.

A cell phone fell from the pack and clattered to the floor.
Bentley took a pair of latex gloves from a pouch on his belt
and slipped them on before examining the tiny screen.

"We'll have the tech guy analyze the call history." He
squinted. "Looks like our Autie is a real texting nut. He's got
three right here from the same person." Bentley frowned.

Isabel leaned forward. They might finally know who was
behind Autie's campaign to terrorize her. "Who?"

He studied the screen and then raised his head. "Why don't
you tell me, Ms. Ling?"

Isabel gaped. "How would I know who has been texting
him?"

Bentley's jaw tightened. "Because the three that I'm looking
at appear to have come from you."

Isabel felt the ground shift under her feet. She tried to
summon up something to say, but all she could do was stare
at him.

Logan stepped in. "What makes you think the texts are from Isabel?"

Bentley did not offer the phone to him. He consulted the screen again. *"Landing. Be there with balance Wednesday.* Wasn't that the day you arrived in South Dakota?"

She could only nod.

"The balance of what?" Logan said, his expression dark.

Bentley removed the last item from the pack on the floor. It was an envelope stuffed with hundred-dollar bills. "Then there's another text. *Deal is complete. Lose my number. I'll do the same. Isabel.*" Bentley tapped the envelope. "What deal is that, I wonder?"

"Bentley, you know this isn't what it looks like. This is too easy. Autie wanted me to find this place. That's why he grabbed Tank. It was a setup."

The officer ignored Logan and stared at her.

She forced out the words. "I don't know how, or why, but I've never had anything to do with Autie and I certainly never sent him a text message or money." The insanity of it roiled inside her until she had to bite her lip to keep from bursting into crazed laughter. "He killed my sister. That's the truth. He killed Cassie."

"On that, we agree." Bentley nodded slowly. "The question is, did you hire him to do it?"

Bentley sent his partner to escort them back to the ranch before returning to assist at the blind. Isabel followed Logan on Echo, trying to mull it over, flip the facts around to make sense of them. She'd gotten nowhere when they arrived back at the house. Logan took the horses to tend to them, and Isabel went into the house to sit down.

Instead, she wandered in little circles in the room where Autie had shown up with his gun, in the place where her sister had birthed her dreams for the future, the spot where Isabel now lived as if it was her own.

Hired Autie? The thought was absurd. Anyone could see that. She loved her sister.

Loved her.

But hadn't even exchanged so much as a phone call until four months prior.

She stared wildly around. What motive could she have for killing her sister?

The idea materialized in her mind like a Polaroid film coming into focus. She had nothing, hardly a dollar to her name. Her sister owned a nice chunk of property in a spot being sought after by developers. There were texts supposedly from her to a killer, implying money had changed hands. She could see where the facts took Bentley. She'd paid Autie to kill Cassie so she could inherit the property. There had never been any witnesses to Autie's threats against her. She could have easily made them all up.

Her head began to whirl and she pressed her hands to her mouth to keep from screaming. Bentley thought she'd had her sister killed. Did Logan? Could he believe it?

He hardly knew her. She was estranged from Cassie. She hadn't set foot in South Dakota until her sister was dead. Of course he could believe it. It cut her like a knife. She could not stand the thought of looking into the clear green eyes of the man who'd saved her mother and seeing ugly suspicion there. Something snapped inside her and she was a scared sixteen-year-old again.

She ran, flinging open the door and tearing down the driveway, feet pounding on the dry gravel, a frenzy building inside with each crazed step.

Logan looked up from closing the corral gate and called to her, but she could not stop.

Blindly she flew into the trees, pushing the branches away

that slapped and clawed at her hair. She had to escape. A sharp twig cut her face as she slammed by. A root caught her foot and she fell, scrambling immediately to her feet and careening on.

"Stop, Isabel." Her brain registered Logan's pursuit, but it did not penetrate.

Run, run, run. Blood trickled from the cut on her face into her mouth and the metal tang burned her mouth. She pictured her sister's blood, spilled out on the floor of the shed with no one to notice, no one to ease the pain.

The truth urged her on.

She'd killed her sister. By running. By leaving.

The branches fought her and the sound of pursuing feet came closer.

"Stop it. Listen to me. Stop running."

She thrashed at the undergrowth until a pair of arms grabbed hold of her legs and brought her to the ground. Fighting and kicking, she tried to free herself.

The hands turned her over roughly and pinned her arms behind her head.

Logan held her to the ground and spoke again and again until the words finally penetrated her ears. "You've got to stop running."

Her breath rasped in sharp bursts, but she could not speak. She was afraid, desperately afraid to see suspicion in his eyes. She turned her face away, crying, gasping.

He held both of her wrists in one hand and reached with the other to turn her face to his. "Stop."

She felt the frenzy lift and despair take its place. "I…" The words would not come.

After a moment, he let go of her arms and gently folded them across her belly. Then he stroked her hair, her shoulders, and wiped the tears that had coursed down her face. "You didn't arrange to have your sister killed. I know that."

His face blurred and she blinked to clear her vision. The eyes were still there, clear emeralds with pure light shining in them, unclouded by doubt. She tried again to speak but he silenced her with a kiss. His lips caught the salt of her tears and offered them back to her.

The warmth of his lips lit a spark inside, kindled many years before, the day he rescued her mother's horse. She let it fill her, surging through her body, and she found herself kissing him back, her fingers twined in his hair.

He stopped for a moment, eyes searching her face, and then he kissed her again, as if he was trying to push the fear aside. She opened her mind and heart to him and let the sensation wash over her and ease away the terrible darkness. Heart pounding, she returned the kiss until they were both breathless.

"It's okay." He eased her to a sitting position. "I believe you, Isabel."

I believe you. She repeated the words over and over in her mind. Though the ground was warm underneath her, she shivered, the fear returning. "I can't believe this. I can't believe it. What is happening to me?"

He crouched next to her and ordered Tank to sit as the dog bounded out of the trees. "Let's go back to the house. We'll talk it out."

She tried to stand, but her legs refused to hold her. He lifted her and she held him around the neck, pressing her face to his neck, the pulse there soothing and steady.

Just hold on. Hold on.

She weighed so little—less, he was sure, than the packs he'd carried on his back while jumping out of helicopters. She was all delicate bones, silky hair…and fear. He knew with a rock-solid certainty she was telling the truth.

On the walk back to the cabin he tried to analyze his own

convictions. She had come to town for the first time, inherited a ranch that could be worth something and told stories about the crazy guy stalking her. It was hard to believe, all right, but the real truth lay in his arms.

Isabel was a victim of a plot, a terrorist who for some reason wanted to destroy her.

His hold on her tightened. Autie would not get the chance.

Logan pushed the door open and sat Isabel at the table. He found a blanket and draped her shoulders, watching for signs of shock.

She clutched the worn flannel and didn't speak.

He opened cupboards and drawers. "How about I whip you up some hot cocoa? My mom always said hot cocoa is the perfect drink no matter what the weather." He dumped cocoa powder and what looked like the right amount of sugar into a pan and added milk, whisking so hard some of the brew slopped over the side and sizzled on the gas burner.

He sloshed some into two chipped mugs and sat down opposite her. "Drink up."

She took a sip and grimaced.

"What? No good?" He drank and forced down a bitter swallow. "Musta got that wrong."

She smiled, and the sight made his culinary flop worthwhile. Anything that erased the terror from her eyes.

She wiped her tear-streaked face and sat up straighter. "You'll have to ask your mother to send you the recipe." She fiddled with the cup. "Do you ever see your mother?"

"Not often. Pararescue kept me away a lot." He swallowed the guilt. The truth was he didn't visit because he was ashamed to talk about his failed marriage and stalled career.

"What does she think about your job?"

He knew Isabel was desperately trying to talk about normal life, to restore some reality back to a surreal situation, but he wished they could talk about the weather or politics. Anything else. "She wanted me to run the family business. My dad owns a quarry."

"But you wouldn't go along with the plan?"

"I'm not a quarry kind of guy. I'll make sandwiches. Hard to mess those up." While he worked, she settled into quiet again. When the sandwiches were ready, he got down to business. "How did Autie get your phone?"

She shook her head, lips trembling. "I thought I left it somewhere or it fell out of my bag. I had to buy a new one."

"Where did you notice it was missing?"

"The airport."

"Okay." He kept his face neutral but she made the connection anyway.

"So…Autie's been after me since I landed here."

"Right. The big question is, how did he know you were coming? Who could have told him that? Did Rawley know?"

"I haven't had any contact with him for years. Only my sister knew I was planning to come here for a visit at some point." She looked down. "I needed a few more months to save up for the trip. But when she died, I got here as soon as I could."

"Autie knew exactly when you were in the airport. Did you call ahead? Tell anyone here your plans?"

"I contacted the lawyer who told me I could stay at the ranch." Her eyes widened.

"Who else?"

"The lawyer gave me the Triggs' number so I could be sure the horses would be tended until I arrived."

Logan tensed. "No. I can see where you're going, but that's the wrong path."

"Why?"

"I've known Sheila and Carl for fifteen years. They're good people."

Her chin went up. "My sister was a good person, too."

"I'm not debating that. I'm just telling you they aren't involved in this. You aren't in a position to know."

"Because I'm an outsider, right?" Her voice was edged with bitterness.

He got up and paced, determined to keep the frustration out of his voice.

"I didn't say that, but the fact is I know them better than you do, so on this point you should believe me. They helped me in every step of my career, and when that went bad they tried to pick me up. I know they supported Nancy as best they could while I was deployed, until..." He cleared his throat. "Until things fell apart. I'm telling you, Carl and Sheila are straight-up good people."

She followed his progress across the kitchen floor. "I'm sure you're right, but you're thinking it, too."

"What?"

Her dark eyes sparked. "About the other person who probably knew I was coming, the person who spent most of his time with Cassie."

He didn't meet her eyes as he stared out the kitchen window. "John Trigg."

"How well do you know him? Is he 'good people' too?"

Logan shrugged. "We never really got along. Never did since high school. I think he's a hothead, and we don't see eye to eye on politics or any other important subject probably, but that doesn't mean he's working with Autie."

"What about his former girlfriend?"

He raised an eyebrow. "What about her?"

"I heard some girls talking. They said she ran away."

"Don't know much except her name. Nora. She worked for Carl and that's how John met her. Then she took off, went overseas, I think. He got even more uptight than he was before. I'm sure Sheila knows more, but it was never my place to ask."

"John's angry at Bentley. Why? And why didn't Bentley arrest him?"

"No idea."

She sighed. "Cassie mentioned that someone close to home was interested in buying the ranch, but she wouldn't sell. Do you think that could have been John?"

He rolled his shoulders against the tension that was building there. "I don't know much about John, but I promise you if he's behind this, we'll find out. In the meantime, we'll have to see what the police and Bill Cloudman come up with. I'll keep them updated."

He returned to his seat. "This is hard for you, all this uncertainty and the accusations. I'm afraid it's going to get worse before it gets better."

She was silent for a moment and he feared she was going to cry again. Instead she stared squarely into his face. "What about for you? How will it be if John really is involved?"

He read the real question. *Will you support the Triggs? Or me?* "I'm not going to toss you out to the coyotes." The color rose in her cheeks, but at least her paralyzing fear seemed to have dissipated.

He prayed it would not come down to John's word against hers.

THIRTEEN

She woke from a nightmare, blanket twisted around her, Autie's voice still floating in her mind.

Disappear.

She jerked upright, heart in her mouth, startled to see Sheila Trigg standing over her, looking surprised.

Sheila pressed a hand to her chest. "You scared me. Bad dream?"

Isabel tossed the blanket aside. "I was napping. I didn't hear you come in." She blinked against the sunlight streaming through the window.

"We heard…there was talk in town. John got wind of some details about Autie's hideout and…Cassie's death."

Isabel noticed wrinkles around Sheila's perfectly lipsticked mouth. One of her fingernails was torn. "Autie's been staying in a hunting blind and I think he murdered Cassie here on the ranch."

Sheila's shook her head. "It's an absolute nightmare."

Isabel took a steadying breath. A nightmare that she would never escape until the truth came out. "Why did you come, Sheila?"

She put her broken fingernail to her mouth. "John was upset when he heard about it. I didn't want…"

"What?"

She shook her head. "He's high-strung. He's had a hard time in relationships. They always seem to turn out to be a disaster."

"Like Nora?"

Sheila sighed and sat down next to Isabel. "He loved her. I always thought she was more interested in his bank account than his personality, but he never saw it that way. When she took off, it really threw him."

"She didn't break things off before she left?"

"No. Not a word." Sheila groaned. "He's as hardheaded as his father. I used to love that about Carl when I thought it was determination. Now it's turned out to be just plain stubbornness. He simply will not see reason about things, and John is the same. It's maddening."

"What happened with Nora? How did they meet?"

She rolled her eyes. "Nora was doing clerical work for Carl. She was new in town, didn't know anyone and she wanted to learn to ride. Carl suggested that John teach her."

"So John and Nora hit it off?"

"They spent every spare moment together until the day she skipped town about a year ago."

"Why do you think she left?"

"I suppose she got a better offer. I know her ex-boyfriend called her a few times from somewhere in Europe. Carl said she used to scurry off to a corner when he phoned. I think she made up with him and ran out, rather than have to make a commitment to my son. Maybe Europe was more to her taste than this hunk of wilderness. Can't really blame her for that." She pinched the bridge of her nose. "It's been a series of downhill slides since then. John's half crazy, Carl drinks, too…" She broke off. "Am I babbling? Horrible. I think I need a long nap."

Isabel saw the sheen of tears in Sheila's eyes. She chose her words carefully. "I can see how Nora's betrayal would hurt John."

"I warned him about her, but he didn't listen. Some things people have to learn for themselves." She looked at Isabel. "Did you ever get involved with the wrong person? The kind of person that everyone else knew was a mistake but you just couldn't see it that way?"

Isabel had to bite her tongue to keep from laughing. The wrong person? She could write a book on the subject. Her heart ached for Sheila, but she remained wary. If John had sicced Autie on her, then Sheila might be unwittingly funneling him information.

"Haven't we all made mistakes like that?"

Sheila gave her a searching look. "Well, I have, but good judgment just doesn't factor into love, does it? I was a social worker in my younger days, and I've seen all kinds of insanity, believe me. People can convince themselves of the craziest things." She drifted to the window and her eyes narrowed. "I'd better get out there. Looks like John and Logan are having a serious talk."

"Are you afraid John will start punching like he did with Bentley?"

She didn't answer.

Isabel laid a hand on Sheila's arm. "Why is John so angry with Bentley, Sheila?"

"Who knows?" she said as they left the house.

You do, Isabel thought.

John and Logan stood outside the yellow police tape. John didn't notice their approach.

"What is going on here? I have a right to know everything, Logan." John's face was flushed and sweat glistened on his forehead under the cowboy hat.

Logan folded his arms across his chest. "You know as

much as the rest of the world. There is evidence in the shed to indicate she was killed there."

"No way. I found her on the trail with Blue Boy running loose. She was thrown. The doctor confirmed it."

"The police will do their thing and we'll know the truth soon enough."

John snorted. "I wouldn't trust Bentley to feed my dog, but he's closed the case and the thing is done."

"Cases can be reopened."

"And why are you so close to all this, Logan? What business is it of yours?"

"The horses are mine. I've got a stake here."

"That's not it." He finally noticed Isabel and Sheila. "It's her, isn't it? You've got a thing for the sister."

Logan straightened. "John, shut up before you get yourself into trouble. I think you'd better quit spouting off and prepare yourself for some questions."

"Questions?" Sheila said. "Why?"

"Because John spent lots of time with Cassie and he was the one who found her body. The police are going to need to interview him," Logan said.

John spat on the ground. "If Bentley comes near me again, I'll break his jaw."

"Not the best approach to prove your innocence."

John's eyes blazed. "Innocence? Quit talking like a cop. You don't know what went on around here. You're an outsider."

"I've lived here as long as you."

"Nah. You left. To do your hero bit. Left everything behind, including your marriage."

Logan took a step forward. "That's enough."

"No, it ain't. You strut around all important, but fact of the matter is, you couldn't even hang on to your own wife."

Logan's eyes glittered and Isabel could see him take a long, slow breath. When he spoke, it was low and deep. "John, I'm not going to take you apart right now because I think you've had a lot to deal with and I respect your parents, but I suggest that you get your facts in order before the police come to call."

Sheila stepped toward him. "John didn't hurt Cassie. It was probably that maniac who's chasing Isabel around."

"Someone hired that maniac," Logan said.

She started. "Who?"

Logan paused. "That's unclear."

Sheila sucked in a breath. "Who do you think, Logan?"

Isabel could not stand to see Logan cover for her, especially with a woman he held so dear. She stepped forward to speak, but someone else answered first.

Carl pulled up in a truck, wheels squealing as he stopped abruptly. He got out, face flushed, sweat shining on his wide face. "Bentley says he found some interesting evidence in the hunting blind."

John raised an eyebrow. "What evidence?"

"The kind that proves Isabel hired Autie to kill her own sister."

Logan took in the surprise on Sheila's and John's faces. He held up a hand. "Carl, that's police business. It isn't for you to be spreading around."

"I'm the mayor, Logan. If I need to know what's going on in my town, I'm going to find out, especially when I hear accusations being leveled at my son."

"No one is accusing your son."

Carl huffed. He looked at Isabel, blotches of color on his face. "So? You hired that nut to kill your sister so you could get your hands on her land?"

Isabel took a step back as if she'd been struck. "No. That's not what happened."

John shook his head. "Then why would the cops think that?"

Carl didn't take his eyes off Isabel. "They got his phone and found texts on it from her. Money hidden in the blind, also."

Logan moved closer to Isabel. "Her phone was stolen at the airport."

Carl snorted. "That's what I'd say too, if I was trying to save my own skin."

John gaped. "Isabel hired Autie? This whole time, all the stories about him stalking her, those were lies?"

"No," Isabel said, her voice pitched higher. "I'm not the one who is lying. I didn't hire anyone to kill my sister. Whoever did is trying to make it look like I am behind it." She glared at John.

Carl laughed. "Prisons are full of people who were framed, aren't they? I just can't see how you could do it. Your own sister. Your only kin."

Isabel wrapped her arms around herself and Logan moved a pace in front of her. "Carl, you're a reasonable man. You know about the innocent until proven guilty rule."

Carl planted his hands on his hips. "Some things cross the line, Logan. Cassie was a nice gal, a sweetheart. It never should have happened to her. She was young and had her whole life to go yet." Tears rolled down his fleshy cheeks.

John looked uncertainly from his mother to his father.

Sheila put a hand on his arm. "Not now, Carl."

He shook his head. "It's not right. A young girl like that, just wanted to care for her horses and be left alone."

John pushed his hat up with a thumb and turned to Isabel. "I always wondered how come you never came to visit, only got one sister and you stayed away. Didn't have the courage to come here and kill her yourself? Had to hire someone to ambush her?"

"No," Isabel whispered. "No."

Logan said, "I think you'd better leave, both of you."

John puffed up. "You don't give me orders."

"Yes, on this one, I am giving you an order. Leave here. Now." John took a step forward and Logan readied himself for a fight. Hand to hand would be no problem with John, but he didn't want to hurt him.

John's eyes moved in thought, fists balled at his side.

They both stood tense and ready until Sheila broke in.

"John, go with your father to the truck. He's been drinking and I don't want him behind the wheel." Sheila's voice was commanding and John obeyed, a look of hatred on his face.

Carl stumbled and Logan reached out to steady him. Carl leaned against him for a moment. "Think about your choices, son. You've finally got a shot to get back into pararescue, don't you? You make the wrong decision, ally yourself with a murderer, and you can kiss that shot goodbye. She's a stranger and an outsider. You can't trust an outsider."

Logan set him back on his feet. "Go home, Carl."

"You think about what I said. Are you willing to bet your dream on her?"

Carl and John went to the truck. Sheila took Isabel's hands. "I'm sorry, honey. Carl gets real emotional. I'm sure when he calms down, he'll realize you couldn't have done those things. It will all be forgotten in time."

Isabel stood stiffly and Logan knew it would never be forgotten in her mind.

Sheila followed the men.

Isabel could have been a statue, standing immobile in the afternoon light, staring at the departing truck. Logan drew closer.

"They're upset, not thinking straight."

"They're right about one thing. You shouldn't be associated with me."

He tried to play it light. "I'm a big boy. I can pick my own playmates."

"It's not funny. Supporting me, especially against a mayor who is soon to be a senator, could kill your chances in pararescue. Isn't that right?"

"Isabel…"

"Isn't that right?" Her eyes glittered.

He allowed the thought to surface. Pararescue would not consider reupping him if there was the slightest hint that he'd become involved in a murder investigation, no matter how innocently. There were too many other soldiers who wanted the job. He knew it, even though he couldn't say the words.

She gave him a searching look and turned away.

"I won't abandon you," he said, catching her by the shoulders. She tried to twist out of his grasp, but he held firm.

"It's not abandonment if I ask you to leave."

Her face was so close. Was this stirring in his soul a warning to leave before he was so entangled he'd ruin his career? *You could lose everything, Logan.* He left logic behind as his hands moved up to cup her cheeks.

He kissed her, surprised that there could be such tenderness in him and that it could find expression with this woman, a memory from so long ago. Her mouth was soft and he moved his lips over hers again. "Are you asking me to leave? Say it then."

Her breath came fast as she clung to him. "I'm asking you to leave. I—I don't want you here."

The words should have hurt, but he felt in the grip of some strong tide washing over him. He was supposed to be here, with her, at least for now. The strength of the feeling tingled through his body. He didn't release her. Instead he traced his lips down her cheek and across her jaw until he came to her ear. "Sorry," he whispered. "But I'm going to have to disobey your order."

She jerked away, angry now, or doing a good job pretending. "I don't want your career to end because of me. You should be packing your bags to get out of here, off this ranch, back to your brigade."

"Squad."

"Whatever you call it."

"I call it a squad, and when they call then I'll deal with that."

"Logan, it's crazy to stay here. The only reason I'm still here is because I have to be, at least until Cassie's killer is found and I can unload this place."

"Fair enough. You have your reasons and I have two tasks to complete here. First, I own six horses that need caring for while I find them permanent homes. Second—" He pulled a coil of tubing from his pocket to repair the backhoe. "I haven't finished the job for Cassie."

Isabel's mouth fell open. "You have got to be kidding. You're thinking about that idiotic ravine in the middle of this madness?"

He grinned. "I do my best work during periods of madness."

FOURTEEN

The following morning, Logan rose with the sun and began tinkering with the backhoe until Isabel emerged from the house, heading for the truck.

He did a double take at her clothing, nice slacks, soft floaty blouse. "Where are you headed?"

"To church. Are you coming?"

He looked down at his jeans and T-shirt. "I forgot it was Sunday."

"God doesn't care what you're wearing. Come on."

She was giving orders now? He put the tools down and washed his hands at the pump. He'd fallen out of the habit of church after he married. Nancy had plenty of reasons not to go, and he discovered the biggest one after they broke up. The wife of the man she was having an affair with was a regular church attender.

He slid into the truck in the passenger seat and they took off.

The people mingling outside stopped their conversations when Isabel stepped out. He saw her press her lips together. "Word travels fast," she said.

"Sure you want to do this?"

"Yes. God is the only thing I've had to hold on to and I'm not letting go now."

Logan's gut tightened to see the determination on her face, the same glimmer of earnest emotion he'd seen that day so many years ago in the barn. She had courage. It was more enticing than the most expensive perfume.

He took her arm and they walked into church together. The Triggs, minus John, were in the front row. Sheila waved at Logan and Isabel. Carl nudged her, a scowl on his face. He gave Logan a meaningful look.

Again he wondered as he caught the surreptitious glances from the congregation, was he risking his future standing beside her? Probably, but for a reason he did not fully understand, he didn't care. Seated in a row close to the back, with her leg pressed against his, the warmth drove away whatever objections his brain could come up with.

After the service, they found Sheila waiting at their truck.

She hugged Isabel and Logan. "Isabel, I wanted to say again that I believe you had nothing to do with the unpleasantness, and I'm so sorry my husband is being such a fool. If I could buy that property from you and set you free, I would, honey, but we've got so much money tied up in Carl's campaign."

He could see Isabel was moved by the offer.

"Thank you, Sheila. Just having you believe me is more than enough."

"No, it's not." She sighed. "It doesn't make up for the gossip, which is no doubt running rampant right this very moment. Listen, if you don't want to deal with this, I can take over your Moonlight Ride guests. We've got two extra horses that can fill in."

Isabel shook her head. "I can do it."

Sheila looked dubious.

"The horses rode very well when we took them out," Logan said. "The couple we're taking is looking to add several to their stable, so it's too good an opportunity to pass up."

"I guess so. In this economy it's rare to find someone willing to take on more than one." She gave him a close look. "You know you've got grease on your shirt."

He felt his face heat up. "I was fixing the backhoe before we left for church."

"Why in the world would you do that?"

"Clearing the ravine."

She stared for a long moment before her face split into a smile. "You two are quite a pair. Nothing fazes you, does it?" A movement from behind caught her attention. "I've got to go. Carl's looking for me. I'll come see you, Isabel, and we can set a date for Cassie's memorial. I didn't forget about it." She gave them both a quick kiss and hurried back toward the church.

On the drive back, Isabel was silent.

"You okay?"

"I was just thinking that maybe Autie took off. You wounded him, the police are searching. Could it be he's disappeared?"

"Nothing is impossible. Why do you sound unhappy about that?"

"The guy's crazy, Logan, but if he vanishes, how will I ever prove that he killed my sister?"

"And who hired him."

"Right."

"You given any more thought to Rawley as a suspect?"

Her fingers gripped the steering wheel tighter. "I don't think it's him, but I could be wrong. He's crazy and vindictive."

"How did you get involved with him?"

She hesitated, then swallowed hard. "I ran away, found myself in L.A. with no money. Scared and lost at sixteen, and there he was. Handsome, friendly, and he kindly gave me a place to stay, a nice apartment. When I came of age, we fell in love. Or at least I thought we did. He kept up the facade for quite a while until I figured out it was all a pretense. He was running a drug ring and he needed a wife to provide cover, go to drops and be places he didn't want to be seen. It took me so long to get wise that by the time I figured it out, it was too late. I was married to him for four years, the worst years of my life. I tried so hard to get away, to get help. The last time I crossed him, he broke my wrist."

Rage coursed through him. "He beat you?"

She bit her lip. "I ran away several times but he or one of his cronies always found me. Then one time I was approached by a man I thought was a buyer, only he turned out to be an undercover cop. He said if I wore a wire, they could send Rawley to jail, and that's exactly what happened."

Logan marveled. "That took some guts, to wear a wire."

She nodded. "He would have killed me if he realized." She let out a breath. "He'll kill me if he ever gets the chance."

"He won't." Logan heard the menace in his own voice.

She gave him a rueful smile. "Autie knew all about Rawley, that's why I figured he was behind it. Autie must sympathize with Rawley, I think because his own father is in jail. But now, I'm not sure my ex hired him anymore. Rawley doesn't beat around the bush. If he'd hired Autie, I think he would have told him to kill me straight out, and so far I'm still alive."

And I'm going to keep it that way. He caressed her shoulder, her muscles knotted tight with fear.

"I was ashamed of myself, the way I left Cassie and got tangled up with Rawley. I couldn't face my sister. I wanted to go back, to call her so many times, but I didn't." She sighed. "I didn't."

Logan wished he had something to say to ease her grief. Instead he squeezed her shoulder and tried to show her in the gesture that he understood.

When they returned to the ranch, Logan kept Isabel in his range of vision while he worked on the backhoe. She moved among the horses easily, as if she was a part of the herd. He'd seen herds accept outsiders, broken and dispirited, integrating them into the family without conflict or judgment. He thought of Carl's angry accusations on the previous day. Horses were more humane than humans sometimes.

The backhoe finally grumbled to life again. Logan lost no time easing it to the edge of the ravine to move the small pile of debris he'd managed to accumulate before Cassie's death. Trip after trip he retrieved the jagged rocks and hauled them away, clearing the way for more to be removed. Sweat poured down his face as the afternoon temperature climbed into the hundreds. Out of the corner of his eye, he saw Isabel stiffen.

Instantly he killed the motor and climbed down.

She ran toward him, eyes wide. "I heard something."

"From where?"

"There," she pointed toward the woods.

Then he heard it, too. The sound of a woman screaming.

Isabel froze, straining to locate the origin of the sound. Logan was already running toward the direction of the tree-covered ridge.

She ran after him, skirting clumps of jimsonweed, skidding on loose patches of red gravel. Logan outpaced her and vanished over the top. She continued on as fast as she was able, until a riderless horse careened out of the scrub.

Her heart sank as she recognized Sheila's mount. The horse stopped, stamping uneasily, head tossing, reins whipping around.

"Here, boy. Here, now. It's okay." She kept her voice low and moved closer.

The horse shimmied.

She reached out a hand and rubbed him gently on the nose until he calmed enough for her to grab the reins. She led him down the slope and tied him to a tree branch before she continued after Logan.

The screaming had stopped.

She paused at the top, staying in the shadow of the shrubs as she had seen Logan do. The murmur of voices was so faint she almost didn't catch it. Following the sounds, she crept as quietly as she dared, stepping gingerly over the pine needles.

Behind a tumble of rough boulders, she found Logan kneeling next to Sheila.

Her breath caught as she scrambled to them. "How badly are you hurt? What happened?"

Sheila's face was pale and a bruise shone on the side of her head. "I saw him. I saw that crazy man."

Isabel suppressed a shiver. "Did he hurt you?"

"No. I was on my way here, to talk to you about the memorial, and I saw him standing under the trees. I got so scared I turned my horse too sharply and I fell off. I thought he was going to kill me, but instead he ran back into the trees."

Isabel's head jerked involuntarily toward the horizon. There was only the unbroken line of green pines and red rock. No sign of Autie.

Sheila struggled to sit.

Logan pressed her back down. "Did you hit your head?"

"I must have, but not hard. I'm okay." She pushed away his restraining hand and sat up.

Isabel brushed pine needles and leaves from Sheila's hair. "I'm so sorry."

"My horse…"

"I got him. He's tied to a tree."

She grasped Isabel's hand. "Thank you."

Logan and Isabel helped Sheila rise and get her bearings. Logan looked closely into her face. "Can you walk?"

She managed an indignant look. "I've been through two mayoral elections and childbirth. Of course I can walk."

Isabel stifled a smile as they guided Sheila down to the cabin, retrieving the horse on the way.

"I'll call Carl," Logan said.

"No. Don't."

Logan's fingers stopped on the cell pad. "I think it would be best."

"No. He's half-bonkers about Isabel in the first place. I don't want to add fuel to the fire, at least until I have to."

Though she didn't say so, Isabel was relieved not to have to deal with Carl and the tension of his presence. While she fetched Sheila a glass of water, Logan summoned Officer Bentley, who arrived a scant thirty minutes later.

He hastened to Sheila's side. "Do you need a doctor?"

She waved a hand. "No, no, Jack. I'm fine, really." She gave him a rundown of the accident. "So you see, I sort of hurt myself, I was so surprised to see Autie."

"Did you see which direction he went?" Bentley said, hand on his radio.

"Toward the Badlands."

The very place they were headed on the Moonlight Ride. She knew Logan was thinking the same thing, though she avoided eye contact. Bentley radioed in the information and then knelt next to Sheila.

"You should go to the hospital."

She flashed him a saucy smile. "But you know I won't. A hardheaded politician's wife such as myself does not need to see a doctor for a little bump."

He laid a hand over hers. The look Sheila gave him was sad, and intimate, the kind of look shared with a relative or...

Isabel almost gasped aloud.

A lover.

It became clear to her in that moment why John Trigg was

so angry at Bentley—because the man had an affair with his mother.

Did Carl know? If John did, chances were excellent the mayor did, too.

Isabel felt uncomfortable.

Logan turned to the window, his face drawn in concentration. Something was bothering him. Had he seen Bentley's gesture? He would not want to see signs of Sheila Trigg's infidelity.

She joined him. "Something out there?"

He continued to stare outside. "No. Nothing that I can see."

"What's wrong?"

He shrugged. "I'm not sure. Let me stew on it awhile and I'll fill you in."

There it was again. Soldier in charge. Information on a need-to-know basis only. She made sure Bentley was still tending to Sheila before she went outside to the horses. They leaned against the fence, ready for a caress.

Logan joined her. "Air get too thick in there?"

She sighed. Why tell him? What was he to her that she should bring it up? A friend? A soldier self-assigned to her hopeless mission? Something deeper? "You pulled your commanding officer card and shut me out."

He blinked. "How?"

"You're going to stew on your thoughts and let me know later, remember?"

His head dropped. "Ah. Sorry. Civilian life is a killer."

She rounded on him. "There's no civilian life or military life. There's only one life and if you keep people out, you pay a terrible price." She was maddened to feel tears start up and trickle down her face. "I wish I had learned it before I lost my sister. It took me too long and then time ran out."

Logan wrapped an arm around her shoulders. "What made

you change your mind and contact Cassie after so many years?"

"A kids' book. Crazy as it seems, I found a torn-up copy of Mother Goose rhymes that my mother used to read to us. I don't even remember taking it when I ran away, but there it was in the bottom of an old backpack. I used to love the pictures. I copied them over and over when I was a child."

Logan rubbed her shoulder and she felt the memory flow out of her, warming and soft like a beloved blanket. "Mom used to make bookmarks for us with Bible verses on them. I found one tucked inside. *'Yea, a little while is the light with you. Walk while ye have the light, lest darkness come upon you.'* John 12:35. It hit me in that moment that I was hiding from the light and the love that God put here for me, wallowing in shame and old pride. I wrote Cassie a letter right then."

They gazed at the horses, silhouetted by a waning sun. He turned her to face him, voice thick with some feeling she couldn't identify.

"I've met a lot of brave people in my time. Men who went into places where they knew they would probably not survive." His eyes searched her face. "But I think you are about the bravest person I've ever known."

"Hardly. I ran away and hid from my sins."

"But you had the courage to face them in the end. Plenty of people pass their whole lives without doing that."

"Are you one of those people?"

His eyes searched hers. "The jury's out on that." His phone beeped and he let go of her. "Got an e-mail from Bill." He read it, eyes widening.

She waited. "Going to stew on it awhile?"

He hesitated for only a moment. "No, ma'am. I think this time you're going to hear all of it, I promise."

FIFTEEN

He was about to fill her in when Bentley led Sheila out the front door.

"I'm going to drop Mrs. Trigg at home. She refuses to go to the hospital."

Sheila waved him off. "I'm fine. Really. I'll send John over for my horse tomorrow. Can you keep him here tonight?"

Isabel hugged her. "Of course. I'm so sorry about what happened."

She smiled. "I'm over it now, but my legs are still a little shaky." Bentley escorted her to his squad car. Logan could not ignore the tenderness in Bentley's treatment. He saw the look on Isabel's face that told him she knew the truth, too.

Bentley returned. "You see any sign of Autie, Logan?"

"No. He was gone by the time we got to her. Did you interview John again?"

"My partner did. He gives the same story, and we've got no reason to doubt it unless the coroner can point us in another direction." He shot a look at Isabel. "I'd tell you to be careful, Miss Ling, stay inside, but you don't seem to have a scratch on you. Autie's never laid a finger on you, has he? Only the people around you seem to get hurt."

"I didn't hire him."

"The evidence will clear you then, but so far it just makes

you look dirty. We're checking your phone records and L.A.P.D. is doing a search of your apartment."

Isabel gave a bitter laugh. "Sheila believes me, and you obviously respect her opinion."

Bentley winced slightly. "Sheila's got a heart as big as the Badlands, but she's practical, too. She knows when to cut her losses. Sooner or later, she'll see the truth and when that happens…" He smiled. "Well, I wouldn't want to be on her bad side, especially if she thinks you had a hand in hurting her son."

He turned to Logan. "You carrying?"

"Yeah. Pistol."

"Keep it handy. Your partner here is in league with a very bad boy and you might catch some collateral damage."

Bentley drove away down the graveled road.

Logan followed Isabel to the house.

"They're involved," she said, flopping onto the couch. "Bentley and Sheila."

"That would explain John's animosity and Carl's drinking." He rubbed a hand over his face, wishing he could wash it all away.

"This is a mess," she groaned.

"And getting messier all the time. Here's the e-mail from Bill." He pulled out his phone and began to read aloud.

"Logan, Autie's father is in prison with no chance of parole for the next decade. Rawley's behind bars, too, no sign of his release and no record of any contact between Autie and Rawley. If I had to guess, I'd say Rawley isn't behind it.

Second point. Looking into the broader circle of participants, aside from Isabel's obvious motive of inheritance…"

He shot her a look. She grimaced, but gestured for him to continue.

"The next best rationale is a lover's spat. Digging into Nora Baker, John's first love, I can find no sign of her. My contacts in Europe turned up empty, too. Man identified as her ex-boyfriend is in jail for car theft and has been for three years. Contacts looking into his part in her apparent disappearance, but nothing so far."

"So, Nora's disappeared without a trace, and the most likely person to have done it is…"

Logan finished the sentence. "John Trigg."

She closed her eyes. "Maybe he made my sister disappear, too."

"And hired Autie to get rid of you when you came around asking questions. When you got too close, they changed the plan and decided to frame you instead."

She shook her head. "Bentley won't dig deep where John is concerned. First, he doesn't want to hurt Sheila and, second, he'd have to cross Carl, after having an affair with his wife."

Logan paced the living room until he slammed his hands down on the kitchen table. "I can't believe this."

Isabel jumped and moved to him. "I'm sorry. I forgot these are your friends. This must be awful for you."

"Carl and Sheila are good parents, at least they've tried to be. If John is a killer, it will destroy them both. How can I watch that happen?"

Isabel traced her fingers up and down his arm, setting his nerves on fire. "I have to continue, but you don't. You can walk away. Please, Logan. Think about it."

He wrapped her in a tight embrace. *Walk while ye have the light...*

There was so much strength in this small woman, so much light. He wondered if she could be the one to share that light with him.

Or leave him in darkness, the way his marriage had.

He forced himself to pull her to arm's length. "I'll take care of myself, but for now I need to tell you something you don't want to hear."

She raised an eyebrow. "Fire away, Captain."

"The Moonlight Ride is Tuesday night."

"Yes."

"You're not going."

She raised the other eyebrow. "I'm not going?"

He started to pace again. "Too many chances for Autie to get to you."

"With all those people around?"

"We're talking a hundred people and horses. Organized chaos. Autie's a local boy. He knows the setup."

"I'm going."

"No, you're not. You'll stay in town. This isn't time for rash behavior."

She folded her arms and stared at him. "You're not my commanding officer."

He grabbed her hand and pulled her to the window. The cliffs rose in magnificent desolation in the distance, cut through with ribbons of scars gouged into the rock. "Look. Those are the Badlands, Isabel. Two hundred thousand acres of nothing. Do you want to ride out there with a man who probably knows every rock and crevice?"

She turned to him, her face calm. "If I have to. We've got two people who might be interested in adopting the horses."

"I'll go. It's not worth the risk for you."

She didn't look at him when she spoke. "When that phone

call comes, Logan, the one you've been waiting for, you're going to leave. You know it, I know it. The only way for you to do that with a clear conscience is to find homes for these horses, and the best way to do that is the Moonlight Ride."

"Isabel…"

"Can you disagree with anything I just said?"

He wanted to, but the naked truth of it was as plain as the massive cliffs of the Badlands. He would leave. The ranch, South Dakota, the horses…and her.

He would leave it all behind when that phone call came.

"No," he said, the words already heavy with the grief he knew was coming.

"That's what I thought."

"But that doesn't mean you have to do the ride. I'll do it. I can manage the horses."

"You're not as comfortable on horseback as I am. You can't manage your horse, plus their two. If one of them acts up, you're going to need backup."

He had to smile. "You sound like you're planning a sortie."

She laughed. "My only plan is to get these horses adopted so we can both leave here with a clean conscience."

"I don't want you to ride."

"You afraid I'll get in your way if Autie does show up?"

"No." He took a long, slow breath. "I don't want to see you hurt."

"You'll protect me, won't you? Isn't that your job?" she teased.

"I'd die trying."

She cocked her head, a curtain of dark framing her face. "Why would you say that, Logan?"

"Because it's true."

"I forgot your pararescue slogan. 'So that others may live,' isn't it?"

"That's right, and you can't teach an old soldier new tricks."
Though he forced a light tone, his heart was heavy. For her,
he would risk it all. *Why?* he wondered. Why risk his safety
and his career for a girl who'd only just arrived? He saw her
again as she was years ago, lovely, her face lit with emotion.
That same girl stood before him now and he knew, right or
wrong, he would keep her as close as he could until it was
time to go.

The Monday morning sun poked its way through an omi-
nous layer of clouds. *Another summer storm on the way,* Isabel
thought as she got dressed and headed to the kitchen for dry
cereal and coffee. The rumble of the backhoe engine told her
Logan was already hard at work. She tried to imagine what
the ranch would be like when the job was done.

The ravine would be cleared and a ribbon of fresh mountain
water would burble through it. Hopefully someone would be
in the market for a quiet country ranch.

The horses would be adopted to good homes.

And Logan would be gone.

Pain rippled through her.

That's the plan, Isabel. The only plan that will work.

She finished quickly and saw to the horses, though Logan
had already given them their feed and water and released them
in the back pasture to graze with Sheila's horse. She wondered
when John would come to retrieve the animal.

She pictured his weathered face, angry and accusatory,
like his father's, but he had another side, too. She'd also seen
him treat the horses with such tenderness and care.

Could John be a murderer? Could a man who professed to
love Cassie really have killed her? The questions continued
to multiply, but where were the answers? Anger and grief
spurted through her and she wished for something, anything,
to take her mind off the situation. With Logan fully focused

on moving the pile of rock and the horses cropping the grass contentedly, she returned to the cabin.

The police had done a search after the evidence in the shed had come to light, but now it was her turn. There had to be something they had missed that would bring some clarity. Isabel determined to take the place apart bit by bit and hopefully turn up any clue that Cassie had been worried or fearful of John Trigg. It wouldn't be enough to convince Bentley, but at least it was a place to start and a way to keep her mind busy.

She began in the spare room that had served as Cassie's study. There was no computer, which made her smile. Cassie was stuck in the age when people made things, did things like write letters instead of trading information across cyberspace. She was a scribbler, and there were dozens of cryptic notes piled on her desk with messages like "seven bags, check for w. nest in barn." Her sister had been an avid journaler as a girl and Isabel emptied the drawers, hoping to find one, but she turned up nothing but paid bills, veterinary reports and a half-eaten Hershey bar.

Paperback romances spilled out of the bookcases, along with a tattered book about the birds of South Dakota and more volumes on the care and tending of horses than anyone could possibly need. She replaced the books and wandered down the hall to the bedroom. She went through the rickety drawers that didn't quite shut properly, finding Cassie's hairbrush, hand lotion, more scribbled notes and a flashlight. In the bottom drawer, her breath caught.

She lifted out a clipped set of papers, brittle with age and blackened on the edges. The top one was a sketch of Buckwheat, her mother's horse. They were the pictures she herself had drawn, the ones her father had piled up and burned. Cassie must have snatched some from the flames and saved them.

Her eyes blurred with tears. They'd battled as children,

watched their mother die and their father disintegrate and, even though Isabel had run away, her sister hadn't stopped loving her. The grief and joy mingled together in the sobs that shook her. She cradled the papers to her breast and whispered to Cassie all the mistakes she'd made, the terrible decisions that had kept her away until it was too late.

When the storm of tears subsided, she looked one more time through the collection of sketches. As she replaced them in the drawer, she saw a rolled paper tucked alongside. She extracted it and spread it out on the floor.

It, too, was a sketch, but in Cassie's shaky hand. A picture of the cabin with a river running behind it. There was a place for people to hook up their campers and several trails drawn in dark ink. The entire rear of the property was an area for the horses to range when they were not in the barn, also inked on the page.

It was Cassie's dream, in black-and-white smudges on the slightly rumpled paper.

"Oh, Cassie. I'm so sorry you didn't get to make it happen."

She would have, Isabel had no doubt, if her life hadn't been brutally snuffed out in the dark shed.

Restless now, she went outside into a wind that whipped the hair around her face. The clouds were thicker, darker. Logan seemed not to notice as he eased an enormous rock into the shovel of the backhoe and pulled it back to join the others away from the ravine.

Tank danced along after the machine, barking and snapping occasionally at the tires, but always quick enough to escape. When the machine dumped its load, Tank investigated the new arrival with a thorough sniff before he trotted back to the edge to continue his supervision duties.

While Logan concentrated on another area, Tank poked his head over the ravine, tail rigid, ears unfurled. With a bark that was drowned out by the engine noise, he disappeared over the mouth of the ravine, down into the uneven rock below.

"Tank! Come back." Isabel's shout did not carry over the noise.

She hurried carefully along the uneven ground. Logan was turned in the other direction, focused on his work. She jogged to the edge and yelled again for the dog, who was pawing at a pile of rubble.

"You're going to hurt yourself. Whatever critter is in there, it's not worth the trouble." She called him again, but he ignored her so she climbed down a few feet. The dog circled out of her reach, continuing to dig with fury.

"What has gotten you so excited?" She eased down another few inches, loose dirt sliding under her feet and raining down on the dog, who continued his frantic digging.

She held on to a tree root with one hand and stretched out the other to take his collar.

"Come on, Tank. I'm going to bury us both in a rock slide if you don't cooperate."

The dog shoved his snout into the pile and emerged triumphant, tail wagging, something clenched between his teeth.

Sick shock shuddered through her.

Tank showed off his prize.

The pale bone could have belonged to a deer or cow.

If it hadn't been adorned with a wristwatch.

SIXTEEN

"You're going to be hard-pressed to blame this body on Isabel," Logan told Bentley with satisfaction. "It's been here awhile from the looks of it, and she was in L.A. with plenty of people who can give her an alibi." Logan tried to quiet Tank, who was now locked in the cabin, with a look. It didn't work. The dog continued to bark through the window, outraged that his hard-won prize was now laid carefully on a plastic sheet where it was being photographed.

Two more officers were going down on ropes to document and excavate the rest of the skeleton.

Bentley didn't answer. He kept his eyes on the bone Tank had found. "A female."

"Most likely. It's a woman's watch."

"Been there about three years, you figure?"

"At least."

Bentley shot a look at Isabel, who was answering questions for a sweaty cop. "Same time her sister bought the place."

Logan nodded. "Let's get down to it, Bentley. This is most likely the body of Nora Baker, John's girlfriend."

"Maybe."

"It's more than a maybe. I don't want John to be guilty either. It's going to ruin his family and they are like my own kin. But the fact is, he's the likeliest suspect here."

"And what? He hired Autie to keep the body from being discovered? Had Cassie killed? The woman he loved?"

"All the trouble started when I began to excavate the ravine. It seems like the most logical explanation."

"And you'd prefer to think it's Sheila's son, rather than the stranger who blows into town in time to inherit a property?"

"I'm looking at the facts and motives."

Bentley's mouth tightened. "How about this? How about you leave the investigation work to me, okay? Facts and motives are my department and, last I looked, you weren't wearing a badge. Stay out of the way."

"I will, as long as Isabel's not being used as a scapegoat."

Bentley scowled. "This whole area is off limits now. The girl can stay in the cabin. You get off the property."

Logan jerked his head at the graveled road. "I'll move my rig a half mile that way, if it makes you happy."

"I said, get out of here."

"As I said, a half mile. Cassie's property line ends there and it's public parkland on that side. All campers welcome."

Bentley's jaw clenched and Logan thought for a moment he was going to swear. "All right. Keep your trailer where it is, but if you get in the way at all, you're going to jail and that isn't going to look good for a pararescueman, is it?"

He stalked off.

Logan made his way to Isabel, who sat on the top rail of the fence. "How are you holding up?"

"I should be horrified, but I don't feel much of anything. I think I'm becoming numb after so many shocks. Do you think that's the body of Nora Baker?"

He raised an eyebrow. "You went there too, huh?"

She shrugged. "The girl went missing around here, and Bill couldn't find any trace of her in Europe. Who else could it be? But does this make things better or worse?"

He had the urge to give her a noncommittal answer, something soothing and bland. Instead he gave her the truth. "To be honest, I don't know. It looks pretty damning for John Trigg, but the fact is Bentley doesn't want to look at that option because of what it will do to Sheila. Forensic evidence may help, but it's been three years." He gestured to the sky. "Three summers of storms and winter freezes. The body may not have much to tell at this point."

"So it's two women murdered on this property and the police still can't pin it on John?"

"Not so far." He took a breath. "However, it does support my earlier position that you shouldn't..."

"I'm going on the ride tomorrow."

"There's a murderer at large. Possibly two."

"If Autie was hired to keep me from discovering the body, it's too late. He failed. Now there's no reason for him to keep after me."

Logan pictured Autie's face, lit with some strange inner fire after Logan shot him. "I can think of one."

She raised a questioning eyebrow.

"Because Autie finishes his missions. He will not accept failure." Logan's insides twisted. "Like me."

"So if he was hired to make me disappear..."

The truth cut an icy path inside him. "He won't stop until he's done it."

Logan walked Isabel inside and returned to watch the search team, sitting far enough away to let his thoughts run their own course. It took him a few minutes to fix on the detail that bothered him. When Autie had scared Sheila the previous day, he'd been standing there, out in the open, watching.

If his mission was to keep the body from being discovered why hadn't he stopped Logan from clearing the ravine? He could pick one of many vantage points and get off a decent shot. One bullet and the work stopped. No one would likely find Nora's body until some future date, if then. If Logan hadn't cleared that ravine, chances are the body would have remained undiscovered indefinitely.

So why hadn't he stopped Logan? Or at least attempted to?

Had the plan changed? What new evil was Autie plotting?

The thought followed him the rest of the day. Before the rain began to fall, the search team cordoned off the area and left with their grisly load, leaving one officer behind to finish up.

Logan watched them go. Was it the end? Nora's terrible death brought to light and John's future come to a horrific stop? Sheila would not let things go gently, he knew. She'd come out fighting and clawing and hire the best lawyer possible if charges were brought. If it wasn't John, then some unknown killer had taken Nora's life and tossed her away like a piece of trash, devastating John and stoking the anger that seemed to perpetually rage inside the man.

Try as he might, Logan could not resolve the crux of the matter. Was John a victim or a murderer?

The next afternoon Isabel tried in vain to take a nap, curled under a sheet, listening to the building wind. It was so like the night she had first arrived, when her life had spiraled into chaos.

No, she thought. That happened when she ran away and married Rawley. Life had only begun to right itself again when she sent that letter to Cassie. Lying there in Cassie's bed, as early drops of rain brushed the window, she felt grateful.

How odd, to be glad to have come to a place where someone was trying to kill her and her sister's murder had been revealed. Yet she was glad, deep down. No matter how it turned out, she had become a part of Cassie's life again, her hopes and passion. God led her out of hiding and reconnected her with her sister through the windswept piece of land that was home to six misfit horses.

And Logan.

When he left, she would feel the loss forever, as she would her sister's.

But she was grateful to have met someone to…

Her heart filled in the rest.

To love?

The idea was too crazy to contemplate. In the middle of a murder investigation with a crazy man stalking her and a herd of horses to tend, it was not the time to have any fanciful notions about love, especially with a man destined to leave at any time.

She got out of bed and left the crazy thoughts amid the tangled blankets, determined to focus on making the Moonlight Ride a success. Logan was leaving and the only thing she could do to make that easier on both of them was to find homes for the horses.

She found Logan at the horse trailer, readying it for the horses that the guests would ride. Len, a volunteer from the Range Rustlers, agreed to drive it to town while Logan and Isabel rode Blue Boy and Echo.

Logan looked up from his work, face serious. He wore a backpack that she knew probably contained his gun. He didn't smile.

"Last chance to make a rational decision here. I can get Len to ride Blue Boy."

"Len hasn't ridden Blue Boy before. It's better for me to do it."

He sighed and handed her a protein bar. "Here. At least keep this with you in case your blood sugar drops."

She smiled. "I'll put it in my saddlebag. Come in for a sandwich. Sort of a last supper."

He grimaced. "Don't even joke about that."

"Do you think the storm is finally coming in?" she asked as they ate ham-and-cheese sandwiches.

"Yes. Rain likely, maybe heavy, but the Moonlight Ride is on, rain or shine."

"Where's Tank?"

"I took him back to the condo. It's a no-dogs event. Too bad, I'd feel better having him along."

Her efforts to engage him in light conversation were unsuccessful. As the sun began to wane, he loaded the horses while she saddled the other two, putting her protein bar and extra water in the saddlebag.

Blue Boy's ears swiveled in anticipation. "Be on your best behavior and maybe you'll wind up adopted," she whispered in his ear. "Don't worry. If they're not great people, the deal's off."

Bold words. How many more chances would there be to find homes for them? Folks weren't going to be anxious to visit a ranch where there had been two murders. She hoped the couple they were meeting tonight hadn't heard any of the rumors circulating the town. Bad enough the whole place was crisscrossed with yellow police tape.

The trailer went on ahead.

Logan put on a hat. "So you'll stay behind me, but close. Any sign of trouble and you yell. Got it?"

"Got it." She climbed into the saddle and they set off through the thickening darkness with an eye on the sky. Unless the clouds dissipated, there would be no moon at all on this Moonlight Ride. They rode at an easy pace to the gathering area, a wide field with cliffs hemming it in on two sides. Logan pointed to a gently sloping trail. "Red Rock Pass. That's our assigned route."

Mr. and Mrs. Spencer Quinn met them. They had the weathered look of people who spent their lives outdoors. Mr.

Quinn wore a battered baseball cap and Mrs. Quinn a down jacket in a sizzling yellow color. They examined the horses with enthusiasm.

"We've got a hundred acres in Wyoming. We take folks on overnight riding tours and we're looking to add to our herd." He stroked Blue Boy and looked at his teeth. "Good riders?"

"Very smooth," Isabel said. "They are all pretty good under pressure."

No need to mention that Echo and Striker had come within yards of a killer near the hunting blind and hadn't taken off at the sound of Logan's pistol shot. She left the couple to their inspection as she caught sight of Sheila standing away from the throng, a phone pressed to her ear. As she walked over, she noticed Carl, slouched in the passenger seat of an SUV parked nearby.

Sheila's face was haggard and drawn. She snapped the phone shut when she saw Isabel. "We heard about the body."

Isabel answered with a nod.

Sheila's voice was almost a whisper. "I want you to know, my son had nothing to do with that girl's death. All this terrible business will be straightened out, but you have to know John is not a killer. He's crushed to hear about Nora."

The darkness concentrated the desperation in her face into harsh shadows. Isabel did not know what to say. "The police will figure it out." With Bentley in charge of the investigation, she had to wonder. "Are you and Carl riding together?"

Sheila shot a disgusted look at the SUV. "Carl is sick. He's going to stay in the car until we return."

Isabel saw the bleary look on Carl's face. Memories of her father surfaced and she knew Carl's illness was the kind that is only found at the bottom of a bottle. "That's too bad."

"Yes." Sheila toyed with her hair. "Are you sure you want

to ride tonight, honey? With all the talk…" She gestured to the crowd and Isabel noticed for the first time that several faces were looking in her direction.

The gossipers could just as easily be talking about the latest discovery in the ravine, which had nothing to do with her and everything to do with John Trigg. She raised her chin. "I'm going to ride."

Sheila flashed Isabel a grin. "You're a tough girl. I admire that. I'd better go saddle up."

On her way back to the horses, Isabel was dismayed to see John Trigg headed in the same direction. She tried to draw back in the shadows, but he'd spotted her and came close, dwarfing her from his seat on the big mare.

He stared at her, jaw working. In the distance, Isabel saw Logan watching them carefully. John bent down a little, so close she could see the black stubble on his wide chin. "I don't know what happened to Nora and Cassie." His voice quivered. "All I know is you are not going to pin their deaths on me."

Isabel's heart thumped faster. She readied herself to run or shout if he got off his horse. "I'm not trying to pin anything on you. I just want the truth."

In her peripheral vision she saw Logan sitting stiffly in the saddle, hands on the reins.

John's voice was rough, hoarse. "Be careful, Isabel. You're making a lot of enemies in this town."

She bit her lip to keep from screaming.

Then he moved the horse away.

Logan relaxed in the saddle, but continued to follow John's progress.

She watched John take his place in the group that would go ahead of them on the trail.

What was that old expression? Keep your enemies close.

John would be riding through the darkness, perhaps watching for an opportunity to split off and circle back behind her.

The skin on the back of her neck crawled, but she marched back with as much bravado as she could muster.

Returning to her guests, she climbed up on Blue Boy. The Quinns needed no encouragement to mount and soon they were headed toward Red Rock Pass. They were one of three groups assigned to the trail. Laughter and shouted conversations filled the night air.

Just as Logan was about to lead the group up the trail into the darkness, he reached for his phone. Isabel watched his face as he pushed a button to retrieve messages. It was a tortured mixture of emotion that she could not fully read in the gloom.

He turned away and listened briefly before stowing it in his pack.

The lift of his shoulders and the quick pace at which he guided his horse along told her what she needed to know.

It was official.

The Air Force would sign him as a trainer.

Logan Price would return to his dreams and leave Isabel alone to build her own.

A sick ache started in her belly. She tried to shake it off.

You knew it was coming, Is.

She had.

But the ache remained anyway.

SEVENTEEN

Logan wished he could dismount and follow Isabel on foot. Instead he was perched on top of a thousand-pound animal with a will of its own. He tried not to dwell on it as he started up the trail, the Quinns behind him and Isabel bringing up the rear. John Trigg was a half mile ahead. Logan liked it that way. Far enough in front where he could keep an eye on him. John was a powder keg waiting to explode.

And what about Autie? He was out there somewhere, too. Waiting.

Logan had half a mind to turn the horse around and throw Isabel over his saddle to get her out of there one way or another. He didn't for two reasons; she'd never forgive him and he didn't have enough confidence in his horsemanship skills to pull it off.

So he gritted his teeth and moved on.

The phone in his backpack pressed into his ribs.

The message from the staff sergeant was clear.

Phone in, Price. Let's talk details.

It was the chance he'd been waiting for since the day his pararescue career had ended in a splintering of bone.

They would let him rejoin.

Thank You, God. You're giving me my family back. Though it was the moment he'd been craving for months, perhaps years, he didn't feel the jubilation that he'd expected from the news. Probably the stress of the current situation.

He turned to check on Isabel. The hair had flown loose from her braid and whipped around her face. She looked so at ease on Blue Boy, as if they were a part of each other. But Blue Boy would be moving on soon, too.

He turned and refocused on the trail. The rain had begun to fall in warm droplets, splattering rocks scored with stripes of ochre and rust, soaking into the ground. Overhead, the clouds seemed to reach down and fill in the gorge into which they were headed, obscuring the moonlight almost completely.

He strained to make out John Trigg in the distance.

The narrow pass was scoured clean by a torrent of water long ago, leaving no boulders or scrub for anyone to hide behind. That was one thing working in their favor, anyway. Still, he wished Tank was along. The goofy dog was likely to get underfoot and pester the horses, but he had a deep-seated dislike of Autie and would know he was around before Logan could.

Logan checked his watch. Almost midnight. If everything went without incident, they would be back to safety by four o'clock. He could return the phone call after the pancake breakfast.

And then what? Would they want him immediately? If the Quinns didn't take some of the horses, how would Isabel tend them herself?

She would do it, somehow. In spite of her life, her troubles, her tragedies, she had reconnected with her sister, even after Cassie was gone. She had a mission and a duty in her own corner of the world that was every bit as important as any he had ever carried out. She would save her sister's dream to give those horses a good home.

The rain fell harder, collecting in little pools that splashed under the horses' hooves. Was Autie out there perched in the rocks somewhere?

The question kicked at him again. Why hadn't Autie stopped him from clearing the ravine? Why watch? And wait?

Logan scanned the darkness, checking the possible ambush points. No sign of anyone.

"How about a stop for pictures?" Mr. Quinn called out.

Pictures were the last thing he wanted to do, but following the "customer is always right" philosophy he nodded and stopped. It gave him a chance to talk to Isabel, who took a few pictures of the Quinns together and held their horses while the couple climbed up a pile of rocks in search of the perfect shot.

He looked around, thinking about another kind of perfect shot.

She punched his arm playfully. "Hey, there. Enjoying the scenery?"

"No," he said. "Too busy watching."

She shivered, and he put an arm around her. "Cold?"

"Not really. Just got a chill up my spine. I saw you on the phone. Was it the call you've been waiting for?"

He wanted to change the subject, but her eyes searched his face with a startling intensity. In that moment he realized another truth. She loved him. He knew she would never say it, with too many scars from her past still aching. But there was love there, the kind of love he'd never seen in another human being, the kind of love that was big enough to let him go. Though he couldn't believe it of himself, he knew he loved her, too.

He stared at the ground, hating himself in that moment. "Yes, it was."

Her voice dropped. "I thought so. I wanted to say that if you need to go before, you know… If the Quinns don't work out before you leave, I can take care of the adoptions. I'm strong enough to handle it."

He squeezed her in the shelter of his arm. "Isabel, you're plenty strong enough to handle it. In fact, you're stronger than I'll ever be."

"Why do you say that?"

"Because you choose to stay in the light. Even when there's darkness so black it can kill you, you stay in the light."

She rubbed her cheek to his hand. "Maybe I had to be in the bad stuff to make me recognize goodness when I see it." She let go. "Anyway, let's get this trip going. I know you have a lot to do when we get back."

The Quinns climbed into the saddle again and they headed toward the narrowest spot on the trail, a place where the rock squeezed in on both sides, leaving room for one horse at a time. Logan's pulse quickened as they approached.

It would be the spot he would pick for an ambush. As casually as he could, he moved his backpack around to the front and took out his pistol, tucking it into his belt. He got the night-scope binoculars and did a thorough scan as they approached the pass. He saw no sign of anyone. The faint sound of laughter from up the trail indicated the group that had gone before them was miles farther along.

He held up a hand. "I'll go first and check to make sure the path is clear."

"Clear from what?" Mrs. Quinn asked.

"Loose rock, that sort of thing," Logan said smoothly.

He eased his mount through the pass, listening for the sound of any movement from above. The only noise was the strike of hooves on the rock. One foot, two. They moved forward slowly.

Three feet, four, five. Then they were through.

The other side of the gap offered little in the way of shrubs to hide behind or good vantage points for taking a shot. With a sigh of relief, he motioned for the Quinns to come through. They did, joining him on the other side, rain collecting on their jackets and dripping off while they waited for Isabel.

Logan stared into the gap, keeping his right hand free to reach for his gun if needed. "Okay, Isabel. Your turn."

Mr. Quinn eyed him closely. "Mr. Price, I get the feeling you're expecting some kind of trouble on this trip."

"No, sir. I just like to be prepared in case trouble finds me."

Mr. Quinn's laughter was lost in the sound of an explosion from high above them.

Blue Boy bucked as the explosion set off a river of rock that rained down on them. Sharp bits gouged Isabel's arms as she tried to shield her face with one hand and hold on to the reins with the other.

The rocks fell faster and faster, loosening enormous chunks that plummeted into the pass. She tried to direct Blue Boy away from the rockfall, but there was not enough room for him to turn. He reared up with a terrified whinny and shied backward, kicking at the debris that thundered down around them.

She clung to him and tried to shout over the noise, but the din was deafening. Blue Boy bucked again as a shard cut his nose.

Isabel couldn't hold on. She sailed through the air, crashing into the side of the canyon. Blue Boy continued to shimmy backward until he came to a spot big enough for him to turn around, and then he galloped down the path and into the darkness.

Isabel tried to get to her feet, but the sliding rock would not allow it. Instead she covered her face and tried to roll into a ball while the land unloaded its burden around her. She was pummeled by a million pieces of flying rock. The cacophony increased to a terrible volume until she thought her eardrums would explode.

The roar tapered off abruptly.

The flow of debris slowed to a trickle.

She remained frozen until she was reasonably sure the ground had stopped its angry tumble.

She allowed herself to peek.

The movement made her aware of a thousand scrapes and scratches burned into her skin. Her shoulder ached from the effort of keeping Blue Boy in check, and blood dripped from a cut on her forearm.

Taking each limb in turn, she moved her arms and legs to check for broken bones. Everything seemed to be working, aside from the trembling that vibrated her body.

She struggled to her feet, relieved to find out her legs somehow supported her. Dust billowed through the night, drifting down in lazy clouds onto the newly fallen debris. Blinking the grit out of her eyes she looked up the trail. The gap through which they had almost passed was completely filled with rock, piled up like marbles in a narrow jar.

The cliffs on either side rose hundreds of feet into the air, hemming in the path on which she stood.

She would not be passing ahead to rejoin the party.

The only choice was to walk back to the starting area the way she'd come and hope to find Blue Boy on the way. She pulled out her satellite phone as she walked down the almost pitch-dark trail.

Her fingers shook as she dialed. The truth, the part her brain desperately didn't want to acknowledge, forced itself to the front.

She knew the explosion was meant to kill her.

Was Autie peering down from the cliffs through his binoculars? Looking for movement in the rubble to indicate she'd survived? Was it John who had caused the explosion? Perhaps he'd assumed he'd killed her and returned to his group.

Pressing herself tightly into the shadows, she dialed Logan's number.

He answered on the first ring. "How bad?"

"Only banged up."

"I can't get through." His voice was charged with intensity. She pictured him, scanning the situation, working out a plan to reach her, and the image brought tears to her eyes.

She started to answer.

A hand snaked around her from behind and pressed the blade of a knife to her throat.

Autie put his face to her ear. "Say goodbye, Isabel."

It must be a horrible dream, a nightmare, but the strong arm holding her shoulders in a viselike grip was real.

Her body went cold. The knife pressure increased until it cut through her thin turtleneck.

When she couldn't utter a sound, he took the phone from her motionless fingers and slid it into his back pocket.

"Well now, Ms. Ling," he said as he turned her around. "It is a pleasure to meet again."

He wore the same soft slouch hat, beaded with moisture, and a buckskin jacket. His chin was stubbled now, making the goatee less distinct. The eyes were no less sharp than she had seen them in the clearing when he had prepared to kill Tank.

"I'll yell. They'll hear me."

He smiled, sliding the knife into a sheath fastened to his belt. "I do not think that will happen."

He would kill her and leave her body for Logan to find. Her legs almost gave out. Instead he reached around and grabbed her by the hair.

She lashed out and kicked behind her, contacting his knee.

Falling, scrambling, she surged forward, but he brought her down quickly.

Breath coming in gasps, she lay on her belly on the wet red earth.

He put a knee firmly on her back. "While this is a diverting entertainment, we really must be moving along." He pulled her to her feet, eyeing her with amusement. "My, my. You are covered in red from head to boots. As if you were washed over in blood."

He laughed again.

She heard voices in the distance, shouts and hoofbeats. Her heart leapt. "They're coming for me."

He moved her down the path at a leisurely pace, turning toward a crevice she had not noticed in the darkness.

"Who, Ms. Ling? Let us be specific then. Who is coming to rescue you? John Trigg? I do not believe he cares enough to cross the street for you."

The crevice widened into an expansive bowl, shielded from above by a lip of rock. He pushed her toward a pile of brush. Her heart sank when she saw an old car concealed under the mat of branches.

Autie continued. "Do you suppose the sheriff will come after you? Perhaps, but he is no challenge, a weak man like that, ruled by his libido."

"Logan," she whispered, wishing she hadn't the moment his name crossed her lips.

"Ah, you're expecting Captain Price. That is quite charming. You believe your soldier will risk life and limb to save you."

She didn't respond.

He jerked her arm, his hand taut with excitement. His words chilled her more than her desperate situation.

"I do hope so," Autie said.

EIGHTEEN

It was all Logan could do to keep from shouting when Isabel's phone disconnected.

"Say goodbye, Isabel."

The words rang in his mind. He already knew who was behind the explosion anyway. Autie had arranged a small charge to detonate at the perfect location to seal off the gorge. That left any rescuers no quick way to get through. Logan paced as he mulled the two choices. He could continue forward for three miles until the trail looped back around, or climb a near vertical cliff, across loosened rock, to make it back across the gorge. Fury swam inside him and he held it in check with brutal effort.

Isabel was alive. He'd hold on to that as he built a rescue plan.

The Quinns were attempting to comfort the startled horses that they'd managed to keep from bolting at the sound of the rockfall.

Mr. Quinn snapped his cell phone shut. "I've reached the group ahead. They're going to turn around and meet us. They'll call for police and rescue."

Logan nodded.

"Do you think…" Mrs. Quinn started. "Do you think she…?"

"She's okay," Logan grunted. "And I'm going to get her."

They both gaped at him. "How?" Mr. Quinn said.

Logan tightened the straps on his backpack and headed for the most stable-looking section of cliff. "Keep Striker with you."

Mr. Quinn shook his head. "Logan, you're going to kill yourself climbing that pile of rubble. Let the rescue people handle it."

He cut across Quinn's words. "Listen carefully. The avalanche was caused by a man named Autie Birch, who has Isabel with him. If I wait, she's dead. Tell the cops when they come."

Mr. Quinn's mouth dropped open, but he nodded.

Mrs. Quinn took hold of the reins. "God help you, son," she said.

I know He will, Logan thought as he began to climb.

The rock at the bottom was fairly stable, and Logan found picking his way upward to be relatively easy. About fifty feet up, where the walls were scoured bare, there were few handholds, and more than once his feet lost contact with the slippery surface.

When a section of gravel slid out from under him, Logan was able to grab hold of an exposed root and hang there long enough to swing his feet up to a protrusion of rock. He lay panting, sandwiched between rock and root, when his phone rang.

It could be Isabel.

Carefully he freed one hand. "Price."

"It's Bill. Where are you?"

"At the moment, I'm hanging from the side of a cliff. Autie has Isabel."

There was a pause. "I just landed in Cheyenne. I'm on my way. Hang on."

"Not funny," Logan said, grunting with the effort of stowing the phone and not losing his grip. A chunk of rock broke off in his hands, sending him sliding a few feet until he managed to find another jagged handhold that saved him from plunging down the cliff. The phone slid out of his fingers and fell, losing pieces as it cracked against rocks on the way down.

No time for regret. The phone was just a tool and he had plenty of those in his arsenal, he told himself.

Hand over hand, he hauled himself up the cliff side, one precarious perch at a time. Just before he topped the crest, he paused to listen.

Autie had planned the abduction carefully, as he'd meticulously mapped out nearly all his attacks on Isabel.

He knew Logan would come after him.

He also knew Logan wasn't the type to wait for a rescue crew or take another, slower trail.

If Autie expected Logan to climb the cliff, he might also be waiting at the top with a rifle to kill him as easily as a gopher popping out of a hole.

Logan listened. He heard nothing but the wind and the distant whine of a coyote. An inch at a time, he eased his head over the top and scanned the dark horizon. Nothing but flat prairie covered by a scalp of grass, still damp from the downpour. He scrambled over the edge and headed for a skeletal pile of rock to his right. From that vantage point, he went still and listened.

The prairie stretched out in a shallow bowl for a mile in each direction before it melted into a rock cliff on either side and what he suspected to be a canyon on the western edge. The Badlands was an intricate interlocking puzzle of tunnels, crevices, cliffs and pockets of trees. Bison, mountain lions and marmots made this wilderness their home.

All of it was wild.

And deadly.

Though he tried to lock down the thoughts, they intruded

anyway. He'd let her get taken. The cops would come, and so would Bill, but they would not be in time. Of all the missions he'd been on, all the times he'd faced desperate odds, this was the one that mattered most.

It wasn't just guilt he felt, or responsibility. A deeper feeling burned through him, heating every nerve and sinew. He shut the emotions down and refocused.

He could not, would not, allow anyone to hurt Isabel Ling, even if it meant laying down his life.

"God help me," he whispered as he took out the night-vision binoculars from his pack. He caught the darting movement of a mule deer cropping the dampened grass. Though the rain had tapered off, the moon was still shrouded by clouds.

His legs itched to run as he pictured Isabel held somewhere in the sprawling prison of the Badlands. Which way? Toward the cliffs? Heading in the direction of the stand of spruce that stood sentinel in the darkness? He felt the beginnings of desperation until he caught it.

The faintest sound that awakened both hope and fear.

The sound of an engine coughing to life.

He shoved the binoculars in his pack and ran for the edge of the crevice, hoping he would not shatter his weakened ankle again, falling into one of the labyrinthine prairie dog tunnels. Pulse pounding, he skirted around rock clusters and pockets of standing water as he raced onward.

He reached his destination. Down in the yawning darkness, he saw the glow of taillights winding into the night before vanishing around a turn.

They would be able to drive only a couple of miles before the rock walls pinched together too close to allow a car. Then Autie would make a decision. He'd kill her there, or head into one of the myriad trails that snaked into the desolation.

Logan didn't stop to hash out the details. He had to get there before Autie ran out of trail and Isabel ran out of time.

* * *

Autie sat in the passenger seat, rifle across his lap. She snuck a peek at his delicate profile. He looked so calm, so sane. Her legs were shaking so badly she could barely press the gas pedal as they moved along. Something told her the only way to survive was to buy some time until someone, Logan or a participant from the Moonlight Ride, had time to reach them. She slowed as much as she dared.

"It's beautiful here, at night," she said, voice shaking. "I guess you know a lot about this place."

Autie gazed out the window without appearing to hear her at first. "Lots of history here," he finally said.

"Have you lived in South Dakota all your life?"

He didn't answer.

"It must have been a good place to grow up, with your mother and father."

His head snapped around to face her, eyes narrowed and anger written in fine lines around his mouth. "You talk too much."

The car bumped along. Rock walls rose up on either side, gouged by centuries of strong wind, sharpened into angular projections that cast eerie shadows in the moonlight. The rock was striped with layers of light and dark, flecks of crystals catching the car's headlights.

She knew enough about the terrain to be properly terrified. Logan's words came back to her. Two hundred thousand acres of wilderness.

How would he ever find her?

And if he did, Autie would be waiting to kill him, too.

Despair flooded through her in waves of black until a hard knot formed in her stomach.

Her life had been a series of impossible situations. She heard her mother's voice. *"In God I shall put my trust, I shall not be afraid. What can man do to me?"*

She gritted her teeth. Autie could hurt and kill her, but she would not make it easy. God would give her the strength to fight, for herself, for Logan, for her sister's dreams. She would go down fighting with her last ounce of strength.

The fear receded just enough to allow Isabel to remember an important detail. The satellite phone was sitting next to her on the seat, where Autie had put it when he got in the car. All she had to do was grab the phone and get away long enough to call Logan and warn him, to hide in this dark abyss for a couple of hours until help arrived.

The clouds formed a thick veil overhead that blotted out the moonlight. Feathery drops of rain brushed across the windshield as the storm kicked up again. The wipers combined the rain and dust into a messy smear on the glass.

She reasoned he would not kill her in the car. He'd force her out, end her life and probably push the car into some solitary canyon. Feigning a look out the driver's side mirror, she ascertained the door was unlocked. When he ordered her to pull under a massive overhang of rock, she knew it was time.

"Get out." Autie reached for the passenger handle, and at the precise moment his back was turned she grabbed the phone and exploded out the door. When her feet hit the soil, she ran with every bit of speed she could muster toward the bluff rising to her left, rain driving into her face and stinging her cheeks.

Her heart thundered in her chest as she ran into the narrow canyon ahead. Autie would be fast, but she had a head start and the rain might disorient him for a moment. Praying as she went, she raced along the uneven ground, tripping on rocks and sliding on patches of gravel until she found herself at a dead end. Ahead the rock folded together. Behind her was Autie with his rifle.

She grabbed hold of the nearest red rock and climbed,

willing herself to become part of the stone that threatened to entomb her.

The rocks tore at her hands, ripping the skin on her grasping fingertips and grabbing at her hair. She didn't stop to listen for the sound of pursuit. A rumble of thunder started softly and increased into a roar that deafened her. She flattened herself against the rock when the lightning came, splitting the sky with an electric sizzle. When it was over, she scanned the area. From her perch halfway up the cliff side, she could see both the gorge below and a glimpse of the prairie that lay at the top of the cliffs. If she hadn't been terrified, it would have seemed majestic, exquisite almost. Watery moonlight painted the whole vista in silver and pearl.

She eased along toward a crevice cut into the rock face a few feet right of her position. She was not sure it would be enough to hide behind. She wondered why she did not hear Autie climbing up after her. Maybe he was not following anymore. He'd given up.

No. There was something in his eyes, the terrible disconnect of emotion that told her he would not stop until he'd completed his mission to kill her. Her mind continued to whirl as she scrambled along. How had she gotten here? Fighting for her life in a barren wilderness? What had she done to deserve the terror of being hunted down like a crippled animal?

Autie's voice echoed in her memory.

"You ran away. You ran from your family and left your father to die.

"Even this place, these endless Badlands, cannot help you escape your own truth."

Before, she would have believed it, let the guilt paralyze her, but the truth flowed through her like a rush of cool water.

She'd come back for her sister who had forgiven her.

She'd met a man who she'd fallen in love with.

She'd chosen to step back into the light, even if it was only for a short while.

Another explosion of thunder, and seconds later came the blaze of lightning. When it had passed she clawed her way to the crevice, hanging on to wet shrubs as she made her way down into the shadows.

Something slithered in the darkness and she nearly screamed. A snake? She clenched her jaw. It was enough to worry about a killer. The snakes would have to stay out of her way. She pressed her back against the rock face, which still held a faint trace of warmth from long hours in ferocious heat. With trembling fingers, she found the phone.

One second to will her fingers to punch in the numbers.

Another moment to clutch the phone to her ear.

A third and she heard only a "caller unavailable" tone.

Then a rifle shot exploded through the air and she felt herself falling.

NINETEEN

The sound of the shot electrified Logan. He sprinted to the edge of the ravine. No movement below that he could detect. The fender of a car showed from under a fold of rock. He found the easiest route and quickly secured a coil of rope around a wide column of sandstone before he began rappelling down. He didn't allow himself to contemplate where the shot might have found its mark.

Or where the next one would.

He raced down, feet springing off the wet rock, lightning illuminating his path.

Isabel would be all right.

And he would stop Autie.

The cliff flashed by in a blur as he made it to the bottom and unclipped himself from the ropes in one smooth movement. Then he was running, weaving toward the car. He crouched behind a fallen boulder a few yards away and checked again for movement.

Nothing.

The strange twisted canyon distorted noise so effectively he could not be sure the shot had come from here or farther down the path, but he could not leave the vehicle unchecked, not if there was a chance she was in there.

Whatever her injuries, he could treat her, save her.

He'd dealt with worse things than bullet holes, he reminded himself.

Heart ricocheting against his ribs, he approached the car, gun in hand. A rumble of thunder thickened the air.

In spite of his slow movements, the grit crunched under his feet with every step.

His mouth went dry as he neared the car. The windows were beaded with a curtain of raindrops but the passenger-side window was open.

He eased around to it, hands squeezed around the gun, body wire taut.

A face appeared.

Logan aimed his pistol as Autie did the same with his rifle.

"Good evening, Captain Price. It would seem that we have a standoff." Autie smiled but the rifle didn't move.

Logan dared not take his eyes off Autie to look inside the car. "Where's Isabel?"

"Isabel? Why, I thought she was with you."

Logan took a step forward. "No more games. Your mission is over. Nora Baker's body has been uncovered, and you and John are going to jail."

"You would not leave a mission unfinished, now would you?"

"I would if we were called off. Consider your mission cancelled and step out of the car."

"But we are just getting started with our little skirmish in the Badlands. Surely you don't want me to surrender already."

"Get out of the car. Slowly."

Autie surprised him by heaving a deep sigh. "Very well, Captain. It seems you have me cornered. I will be a cooperative prisoner. May I offer you the rifle, as terms of my surrender?"

Logan tensed as Autie carefully turned the rifle and handed the butt end to Logan. He took it and backed up a couple of steps to lay it against a rock. "Now, get out and keep your hands where I can see them."

"Of course."

Logan watched Autie exit the vehicle, hands in the air.

Logan's instincts prickled. He smelled an ambush, but Autie patiently let Logan pat him down with one hand.

"No guns or knives up my sleeves, Captain. It's just me and you. That's the best way, is it not? Man against man. An equal playing field."

"Get over here, away from the car."

"Ah, yes. The car. You would want to check that, to be sure Ms. Ling is not folded in the backseat or the trunk, bleeding to death."

"Move." Logan kept the pistol trained on him as Autie backed away, hands still in the air.

"Do you have the time, Captain?" Autie asked.

Logan ignored the question as he made his way gingerly around the car. She was not in the front seat. A pile of blankets obscured his view of the backseat. He hardly noticed Autie's babbling.

"I have a keen sense of time, much like General Custer himself."

"You're not Custer," Logan snapped. "You're Oscar Birch and you're not working on some noble cause. You're a criminal like your father." He eased open the back door, keeping Autie in his peripheral vision.

"That was most uncalled for. I do not believe I have ever slung insults at your family." Autie's tone was cold. "It hardly matters at this point. As I was saying, I have a keen sense of time, and I would estimate it's been nine minutes since you heard the shot and made your way down here with impressive speed and skillful rope work. Would you agree with my estimate? Nine minutes?"

Logan reached one hand in to pat the blankets, skin gone cold at the thought of what he might find there. He felt nothing, so he reached in farther.

"Yes," Autie continued. "I would imagine it to be approaching ten minutes right about now."

Logan's fingers closed around a familiar shape that took him a moment to place. He saw Autie's smile, laced with anticipation, lit by a sudden flash of lightning.

Logan had been right about the ambush.

The last few seconds on the timer ticked away.

Somewhere in her pain-fogged mind, Isabel heard an explosion. Perhaps it was another round of thunder. Autie's shot had grazed her shoulder, causing her to drop her phone into the abyss. The pain was intense, and a warm sensation told her she was bleeding. With gritted teeth she ripped a sleeve from her jacket and tied it firmly around her shoulder, using her teeth to pull the knot tight. Then she crawled under a sheltering rock to catch her breath.

She couldn't stay here. Autie knew her location and he would be after her. She allowed herself one more minute to steady her breathing, and then she crawled out of her hiding place into the stinging rain.

From rock to pointed rock, she made her way along the cliff like the bighorn sheep she knew made this area their home. She supposed she should be terrified, but the blood that seeped from her wound seemed to take the terror with it. Now there was only numbness and the overwhelming need to move on, keep going.

She guessed it to be about four in the morning when the rain finally stopped, leaving her sodden and cold, teeth chattering. The sun would be up in a few hours. As enticing as it was to think of the warmth it would provide, she knew it would also take away her only defense. Autie would be able to spot her quickly as she moved clumsily along, without even a phone to call for help.

She crawled up to the base of a bizarrely twisting hoodoo that gave her a view of the terrain.

It offered few choices.

An endless vista of moonlit spires and cliffs stretched in all directions. Below was a pocket of ground thick with trees, and she concluded it could be Century Grove, one of the stopping points on the Moonlight Ride. Instinct told her to head for the trees rather than risk more climbing than necessary. The light was not sufficient to show her the uneven ground and twice she fell, tearing her pants and causing her shoulder wound to start bleeding again.

It was foolhardy to continue. She would have to wait for predawn and take her chances on being spotted.

Muscles groaning, she tucked herself under an outcropping of rock.

The night seemed alive with noises. Some she recognized, coyote and the whine of insects.

Some she did not. Strange whispers and the scuttling of night creatures she didn't want to contemplate. Her mouth was raw and dry, her water still in Blue Boy's saddlebag. When her stomach growled, she realized the impact of being separated from her supplies. She could survive hungry, but if her blood sugar dropped too low, she would be at risk of losing consciousness.

Lord, help me. Help me out of this terrible place.

She thought of Logan and, though she hadn't seen a glimpse of him, she knew he'd heard the shot and he was out there, coming for her.

I do hope so, Autie had said.

The thought chilled her further. Autie relished the game,

the mission. He would draw Logan out, using her as bait, and kill him.

A lump formed in her throat and she bit her lip until she tasted blood.

The only way to help him was to try to somehow find her way back to one of the Moonlight Ride groups and call for help. Or get out into the open if a search plane flew over. Eyeing the jumble of columns slicing through the air above her, she doubted anyone would spot her.

In books she'd read that people started signal fires, but she hadn't the faintest idea how to go about doing that in this sodden territory. She pulled her good arm around her knees and tried to warm herself.

If she just had a phone, she could call Logan, warn him.

But he would come anyway, just as she would do for him.

The thought gave her comfort as she pictured his green eyes, the laugh lines around his mouth.

Be careful, Logan. Stay alive.

Sleep was unthinkable. The time ticked away in an endless freezing passage until the sky lightened from black to slate-gray. Isabel forced herself to her feet. Her limbs felt wooden with cold, and fiery pain shot through her shoulder.

Her stomach reminded her she hadn't eaten in a while. Patting her pockets, she found only a package of peanuts. She ate a few, hoping the protein would be sufficient to stabilize her blood sugar, and carefully refolded the package.

The ground was still damp, the towering spires around her sparkling with drops of dew. From somewhere close by, a bird started up a repetitive bell tone that set her nerves on edge. The Badlands was awakening and Autie was, too. She tried to hurry, but her clumsiness hampered any quick movement.

One foot more, another step or two, she counted the ago-nizing progress in inches. The almost risen sun painted the rocks in strange shadow and, with a terrible rush of fear, Isabel realized she was disoriented.

Spinning on her heel she saw behind her only the same twisted pillars rising up, caging her in. The rock blocked her view of the panorama and she had no idea which way led to the pocket of green below.

Tears started in her eyes and her breath burned in her lungs. She forced her mind to stop reeling and considered what Logan would do. Her destination had lain to the east. All she had to do was wait for the sun to rise and head that way.

The minutes passed painfully until the first beam of sunlight broke across the horizon. Isabel wasted no time in plunging downslope toward that rose-colored light. She came to a large hoodoo barring her way. The eerie stone bore an almost human form, the chunk of rock resting at the top defying all odds of gravity. Gingerly, she drew to the very edge of it. On one side was a sheer wall that she could never hope to climb. On the other, a narrow ridge of rock that fell away into an uneven slope, dotted with jagged rocks and scrub.

Clinging to the hoodoo, Isabel began to inch around along the ridge, pressing her body to the damp rock. She dared only creep, shards of sandstone pulling loose under her feet and rolling down. The rough surface dug into her face, but she kept her cheek pressed there, embracing the rock as best she could.

The sun burst forth in full glory and her eyes were momentarily dazzled by the glow. There were only about ten steps more. Her outstretched fingers touched something that might have been branches.

A blackbird shot out of a crevice, screaming at the disruption of her nest.

Isabel jerked backward and the movement was enough to send her tumbling.

Pinwheeling faster and faster she tried to spread her arms and legs to slow her descent, but she continued to slide, cascading on a carpet of falling debris until she lost consciousness.

TWENTY

Logan continued to chide himself as he applied pressure to the wound on his forehead. *Dumb, Logan. Almost getting yourself blown up by a guy who thinks he's General Custer.* Autie was crazy, but smart, just like Bill had said. He knew exactly how long to keep Logan talking until the timer reached zero and the dynamite detonated. He'd been outwitted, plain and simple.

Only Logan's surge of adrenalin got him far enough away from the car as the bomb exploded. He must have been out for a while, because it was now sunrise and Autie was gone. With a start, Logan realized his gun was, too. At least Autie had left him the backpack. He wiped off his face as best he could and drank some water from a bottle in his pack. Did Isabel have any water with her?

He looked at the sky, ripe with the promise of an August scorcher. The temperature had dropped low enough in the night to have made her uncomfortable, but not enough to induce hypothermia. It was the heat that would be deadly if he didn't find her soon. Rising slowly to fend off a wave of dizziness, he moved past the burned-out wreck of the car and into the canyon, wishing again that Tank was with him. The dog wasn't any good at following directions, but he had a nose that wouldn't quit.

Logan moved toward the location he thought he'd heard the rifle shot the previous night. The rocks had nothing to tell him. Struggling with a surge of frustration, he started to turn around when he noticed a pile of fallen rock. The pieces lay in a mound, still sharp, showing no signs of weathering to indicate they'd been there for any length of time.

He got out his binoculars and traced a path directly upward from the pile.

The stain of something had dripped down the rock, no more than a spot or two, but clear in his high-powered lenses.

Blood.

His gut tightened.

Stowing the binoculars, he climbed.

By the time he reached the spot where he found the bullet imbedded in the rock, the temperature was already approaching ninety. He worked out the scenario in his mind. Isabel had gotten free of Autie somehow, made a run for it and he'd shot her. She was bleeding, scared. She must have tied up the wound with something because the blood trail tapered off. Either that or Autie had caught up to her.

Somehow, he didn't think so.

The shot had happened around 1:00 a.m., and fleeing into the Badlands in pitch darkness would be impossible. She'd holed up somewhere, he was sure of it.

Hope surged inside him.

There were many routes ahead that crisscrossed and some ended abruptly, but only one offered significant cover from the cliff for the first couple of miles. He moved as fast as he could, considering as he went.

By now, the Moonlight Ride participants would have summoned the police and the Tribal Rangers, who would mount a search and rescue. Civilian volunteers would be limited, since Mr. Quinn had no doubt filled in the cops on Autie's deadly intent.

He checked his watch. 9:00 a.m. Bill would have had time to get from the airport to the Badlands by now and the man was an excellent tracker, but Logan couldn't stop himself from wondering.

Would help reach them in time?

He cut off the doubts.

Doesn't matter. I will find her and keep her alive.

Picturing her wounded and terrified was more than he could deal with, so he quickened his pace. Sweat poured down his face, stinging the laceration on his forehead and washing grit into his eyes. He didn't dare put on sunglasses in case the glare gave him away. Shade was nonexistent here, except for small pools created by the rocky monuments that rose around him.

A movement from the cliff wall ahead tipped him off before he heard the deadly sound carried along by the thin air, and dropped to his belly.

A bullet skimmed past his shoulder and drilled into the rock behind him, the report of the gun echoing madly through the canyon. Instinctively, he reached for his own gun before he remembered Autie had taken it.

"You are a worthy opponent, Captain Price," Autie yelled from someplace deep in the shadows. "I am impressed that you have survived to this point. I could have killed you after the car bomb, of course, but you provide such good sport."

Logan eased back toward the rock and tried to pinpoint Autie's location.

Probably behind a pinnacle of rock at the top of the trail. There was no way Logan was going to be able to circle around and take Autie by surprise.

Another bullet zinged into the ground, sending up a puff of dirt.

"The level of training they give to you and your pararescue

brothers is impressive. Still, I find you in my crosshairs yet again. Perhaps you need a retraining session, Captain."

Logan shimmied back farther until a sharp ridge of rock pressed into his spine. Autie had ammunition galore, he was sure. There was no chance Logan could retreat without being picked off as he did so.

"Captain Price?" Autie's voice was louder now. "I will offer you the honorable way out. If you surrender, I will be happy to kill you quickly instead of hunting you down like a rabid cur. Consider it a sign of respect from one soldier to another."

"Respect this," Logan muttered. Gritting his teeth, he slowly unzipped his backpack and removed a metal cylinder. He mentally calculated the distance and took a deep breath before he pulled the ring. The smoke grenade sailed through the air in a neat arc. It landed with a clatter just behind Autie's hiding place and the yellow haze surged out with a hiss.

Logan didn't waste time. He ran up the trail holding his breath, just ahead of the smoke screen, leaving Autie to fight his way past the stench of terephthalic acid.

It would buy him minutes, five at the most.

He plunged on as fast as he dared along the uneven ground until his way was barred by a hoodoo. The ground next to it had given way.

He read the signs, the fallen rock, broken vegetation.

She'd tried to wriggle past and fallen.

He risked a moment to scan the area with his binoculars, but since the ground dropped sharply out of sight, he could not pinpoint her location. With no more time to waste, he took off down the slope, following as best he could the trail of disturbed ground.

The sun was fully overhead now, baking the rocky surface.

He cast a quick glance at the summit from which he'd

come. The choking smoke was clearing now, wafting up into the sizzling blue sky. Autie would be coming soon and he would be angry at being tricked by the smoke bomb. Logan ran now, scanning in every direction as the sign of Isabel's passage grew fainter with every step. Soon it had petered out altogether, swallowed up by a rugged layer of broken rock. He found himself caged in by a forest of knobbed pillars. Far below, he knew, was a bowl-shaped depression of grassland and trees. She'd have headed there, he thought, but probably did not have the strength to make it.

Breath heaving, he made a tight circle. Her tracks seemed to have vanished, but pressed into the soil he found the unmistakable prints of a mountain lion.

The animals were skilled hunters. Silent and deadly, much like Autie himself. His pulse edged up a notch.

Find her, Logan. Find her.

He kept looking, peering into any crack or crevice that might be big enough to conceal her.

She was hiding, he desperately hoped, not unconscious from blood loss or hypoglycemia. He kept his eyes off the mountain lion tracks. Or worse.

Fearing he'd alert Autie to his location, but running out of options, Logan called her name.

"Isabel? Where are you?"

A sultry breeze teased him and a fat lizard scuttled by his feet.

He tried again, in a louder tone. "Isabel, honey, you have to help me find you. Tell me where you are."

At first he thought it was the wind, playing with his desires. Then the sound repeated itself.

"Here," came the ragged whisper. "I'm here."

Isabel lay in a tiny cave bored into the rock by water that had long ago disappeared into the desert's unforgiving sand.

The heat from the gravel underneath her and the rock pressed into her back felt as though she'd crawled into an oven. She wanted more than anything to escape the burning, but she could not move. Her legs were two useless things and her head spun. Still she heard, or thought she imagined, Logan's voice calling to her.

"I'm here," she called, throat so parched that it came out as a croak.

The effort used up her energy and she closed her eyes.

A hand touched her arm tentatively and she found Logan kneeling over her.

"Isabel, I'm here."

He pressed a bottle to her lips and she thought nothing had ever tasted as delicious as that sip of warm water. Still, she wondered if she was imagining his presence.

"Tell me where you're hurt."

"Just my shoulder, but I'm all wobbly."

He eased her into a sitting position and his green eyes swam into view. The intensity in them drilled into her. He stared at her, eyes roving, until he finally pressed his face to hers, lips tracing her cheekbone.

"I thought I might be too late."

She tried to answer through an onslaught of tears. "Autie put me in a car. I tried to call you, but he shot at me." She grabbed his hand. "Oh, Logan. He wanted you to follow so he could kill you, too."

Logan rummaged through his backpack. "He can take his best shot, but he won't win."

She felt a thrill of terror. "Is he still out there?"

"Yes." Logan removed a protein bar from his pack. "Close. We've got to get you stabilized and out of here."

He unwrapped the bar and handed her a chunk.

The thought of eating was detestable, but she managed to get it down and drink another few sips of water. He turned and she caught his profile. His hair was matted with blood, a gash showing blue-black on his temple.

"You're hurt."

He shrugged. "Own fault. Autie planted a bomb in the car and I didn't catch on quick enough. Must be getting rusty."

Her tears flowed in earnest then. "Logan, you never should have come for me. Never even gotten involved in this mess."

He took hold of her hands and squeezed. Hard. "I'm only going to say this once because we don't have time. There is no place that I would choose to be right now except by your side. Got it?"

No words came. She clung to his fingers and blinked back the tears.

"Can you stand?"

"Yes." She wasn't sure at first she could deliver on her promise. Her legs were as unruly as a new colt's, but she made it, clinging to him as she swayed before regaining her balance.

Logan crouched at the cave opening, staring fixedly at the horizon. "He'll know we're making for the green because that's our best chance of getting help. There's a trailhead there. We're going to have to go about it the long way." He pointed to a route that took them through a path heavy with tall desert grasses and fallen rock. "We can keep some level of cover there. Ready?"

"Ready."

As quietly as they could manage, they scurried out into the harsh sunlight, which dazzled her eyes for a moment. Keeping hold of Logan's hand, she followed blindly.

Her earlier words came back to her. *Never trust a man again. Especially a handsome man.* And that was precisely what she was doing. Furthermore, she knew it was exactly right. She trusted Logan with her life.

And her heart.

Trying to keep the pace without stumbling, she wondered if they would encounter Autie waiting around the next pile of rock, rifle at the ready. He'd been one step ahead of them and now they were in his playground.

She focused on moving her weak legs forward. Each yard they covered seemed to be hotter than the last, until finally he pulled her into the shade of a low cliff and told her to drink. He was sweat-soaked and a little pale, she thought, pushing the bottle back to him.

"You drink. You haven't had any."

He waved it away. "I'm fine. Drink."

She took a small sip and recapped the bottle as the truth dawned on her. The meager half-full bottle was all the water they had until they were rescued.

Or Autie found them.

Stifling a shiver she followed him as the path sloped down into yet another depression of bone-white rock. Logan climbed over a low boulder and turned to offer her a hand. As she crossed, her foot knocked loose a rock that fell with a thud onto the path. The rock rolled past a small hole in the ground and a stream of wasps jetted out in an angry line. Jabbing, retreating and jabbing again, they swarmed around until the air was alive with them, the furious buzzing deafening.

She screamed and held her hands up to protect her face.

They buzzed around her, stinging repeatedly, entangling themselves in her hair.

Trying to bat them away seemed only to enrage the wasps more as they enveloped her body in a humming cloud. Panic surging, she started to run until Logan caught up with her and she'd gotten enough distance from the horde.

He pulled her into some meager shade and slapped the insects away, yanking off the ones who continued their relentless stinging, disentangling the few who had burrowed into her hair. When it was finally over, her arms were punctured in multiple places, her face on fire from the wasps that made contact there.

Logan wetted a section of gauze with the precious water and she pressed it to the worst of the stings.

"Are you allergic to insects?"

She shook her head. "No, but I wish they were allergic to me."

His smile was tight and she looked more closely into his face.

"I'm sorry," she mumbled. "I didn't even see that hole in the ground."

He shook his head wearily. "I didn't see it, either. Focused on other things."

The realization hit her like a vicious stinging thing. Her scream had not scared the wasps in the least. It had done something far worse—revealed to Autie their exact location.

TWENTY ONE

Though he continued on, urging Isabel forward, Logan knew there was no way they would reach the green before Autie caught up to them.

The Badlands hemmed them into a raised plateau, a section of rugged rock scorched by water that had long ago been sucked away, ravaged now only by the wind and the relentless sun. Isabel was weak, moving slowly.

Autie would catch them. It was just a matter of time.

There were only two options. Stay alive until help found them, or take Autie down.

Autie, he knew, was likely to find a location above them on the rim of the plateau where they'd run after the wasp attack. He'd wait patiently. Fully armed, with enough food and water to sustain him. Sooner or later, Logan would have to move to avoid encountering the mountain lion or to seek better shelter when night fell.

The time was almost five and already the shadows were lengthening, the heat at its most intense. As hot as they were now, in a few hours the temperature would plunge. He eyed Isabel where she sat, eyes closed.

Her face was pale, skin marred by wasp stings. The bandage on her shoulder showed signs of fresh blood. Unzipping his pack, he crawled to her, easing off the sodden strip of fabric.

Her eyes found his. "Putting on your doctor hat?"

He didn't like the faintness in her voice. Pressing the water bottle to her parched lips, he made her drink. "Just going to redress the wound. Then we've got to move again."

"Where?"

Anywhere, just to buy time and stay alive until help came. He figured it was best not to tell her about the grim reality, but something in him felt different now. She was not a mission, nor a civilian. She was a woman who had survived more than he could ever understand. A woman of strength and generosity that took his breath away. A woman he loved and would not lie to.

He stroked her cheek. "We're pinned down here, honey. The best we can do is keep moving until help arrives. If I get the chance to take Autie out, I will, but he's careful."

She blinked and then gave him a smile that melted his heart.

"Thank you for being honest with me."

He sighed. "I don't know why, but with you, I want to be completely honest, to show you who I am. Even the not-so-good parts. I guess this old soldier is trying to learn some new tricks after all." He gritted his teeth. "Why can't I get you out of this? I've completed hundreds of successful missions. Why can't I rescue you?"

She reached for his hand. "You already have."

He brushed his lips to her forehead, burning hot. Helplessness welled up again. Autie would hunt them down like animals until he made the kill. For Logan, it was the end he'd been preparing for his entire career, the one he knew lay just beyond the next downed airplane, or hidden inside some nondescript burned-out shell of a house.

But Isabel?

She should not pay this kind of price.

He murmured a silent prayer and laid down his pride. *Help me, Lord. I can't save her, but You can.*

The thwop of a helicopter engine cut through the stillness.

Logan's heart leapt. "It's a police chopper. They're looking for us."

His mind raced. Autie was watching. If Logan stepped out to signal the chopper, he'd be a dead man.

If he didn't, the aircraft would likely pass by and move to another search grid.

Their lives were ticking down to the final minutes. No water, Autie closing in, Isabel weakening.

He felt her grip tighten on his hand, bringing him back.

"Logan, I know what you're thinking. If you go out there, Autie will kill you."

"If I don't, they won't find us in time."

She clung to his hand until her fingers dug into his. "Please don't do it."

"It's going to be okay."

"No, it's not." Tears started down her face. "Not if you die. Not if you give your life for mine. Since that day I saw you so many years ago, some part of me has known that I needed you. You can't go out there to die. I won't let you go."

"Shhh. I have to get us help."

"No," she whispered. "Please."

He kissed her gently on the mouth. "You've taught me so much about what is really important in this life. I love you, Isabel, and I have to do this."

She opened her mouth to reply, tears flowing freely, but he did not wait to hear.

He turned quickly and, crouching low, he ran.

* * *

Isabel cried out but Logan was already gone. Gathering up what little strength she had left, she crawled out of her hiding place. No plan formed in her mind. No goal other than to find Logan and stop him.

She'd lost Cassie, without the chance to tell her how much she loved her.

He would not go out and die, not without knowing that she loved him, too. Desperately. Mindlessly. With a love so pure and light, she knew it came straight from the Lord. It was a sweet emotion, unclouded with the guilt and terror that had driven her into Rawley's trap.

Autie couldn't take him away from her.

Knees shaking, she made it to her feet and lurched out of the shelter.

The chopper was lower now, flying in wide circles over the blistering landscape, whirling the red earth into eddies of rust.

She strained her eyes, desperate to catch sight of Logan, to stop him.

Half-blinded by the sunlight streaming over the cliff tops, she grew dizzy. Forcing herself in the direction she figured he'd gone, she half ran, half staggered. He would head to the highest point, she thought. A place to signal the helicopter.

A tiny blur of movement caught her eye. A figure moved at a quick pace through the rock. She caught no more than a dart of shadow. Was it Logan? Or Autie?

Before fear could override instinct, she took off toward the movement.

Logan climbed the twisting path to the highest point on the plateau. He'd have a moment to fire off the signal flare, and a few more to try to conceal himself until Autie showed up. He'd be an easy target with no escape route.

An idea formed so quickly he didn't have time to think it through. Passing a sharp turn, he pulled out his sunglasses and wedged them into a hollow of rock. Continuing around the corner he checked the line of sight. Perfect. He would see Autie coming just before he rounded the corner. It would buy him only the tiniest bit of surprise, but it would be enough.

It had to be.

He moved on a few more paces before he knelt to extract the signal flare from his backpack. With ten thousand candle-power and a six-and-a-half-second burn time, the signal should alert the chopper. He hoped so, because Autie would be onto him before he had a chance to deploy the other three he'd brought along.

He loaded the flare and aimed, releasing the missile into flight.

His hope soared with the projectile, as it arced three hundred feet into the air in a blazing trail of light.

Lord, let it be enough.

Isabel's breath caught as she saw the plume of fire cut through the air. He'd done it. She watched in terrified fascination as the chopper slowly turned, like some ungainly flying insect. It swiveled to the right and left, drawing closer, and then inconceivably moving away. Her heart filled with hope, but the chopper did not come closer to rescue them. Had it not spotted the flare? Were her eyes playing tricks on her?

It didn't matter now, she realized. Autie most certainly had seen it and was heading for Logan.

She stumbled on, hands grabbing at the rocks as she pushed herself forward. She wanted to scream his name, but her mouth was so dry only a rough bark came out. From somewhere she heard the sound of feet crunching across the gravel.

* * *

Logan flattened himself against the boulders, ignoring the sharp points that cut into his back. He kept his eyes trained on the sunglasses he'd wedged into the rock. They reflected nothing back at him yet, but he'd heard it, the tiny snap of a dry branch.

Autie was on his way.

It was too late to reposition himself. Even a slight movement would reveal his location. With no gun, he was going to have to do it the hard way. On some level, it pleased him. If he could disarm Autie, they'd go hand to hand, the way a fight was supposed to be. No weapons, just strength and cunning and, most importantly, will.

Logan knew he had Autie beat on that score.

His win would ensure that Isabel would live.

Bring it, Autie. I'm ready for you.

She kept running, plowing over the uneven ground, heedless of the sweat that ran into her eyes. Memories of her sister urged her on, giving strength to her battered body and tattered spirit. She thought idly of Blue Boy.

Would he find his way home? She prayed the Lord would lead him back, if not to her, then to people who could care for him, nurture him and help him forget the abuse he'd suffered. She fell heavily on one knee, hands pressed to the hot surface.

Her mind seemed to slow, thoughts turning in on themselves as she moved on, crawling now, without the strength to rise.

Yea, a little while is the light with you. Walk while ye have the light...

Though she'd known Logan only a short while, she knew the Lord brought him into her life to give her light and push away the darkness. The moments with him washed away the years of grief and shame, restoring her heart in a way she'd never imagined possible.

I love you, Logan. Tears started down her face, dotting the ground between her hands as she continued to crawl.

I love you.

The ground burned her hands, blistering the torn skin.

She felt a vibration under her fingers, the ground trembling though she could not be sure it wasn't her own body short-circuiting.

As she struggled to stand, a hand grabbed hold of her arm and kept her pinned to the ground. The thin desert air snatched up her scream and whirled it away.

Logan resisted the urge to wipe the sweat out of his eyes. Any sound, any shadow would alert Autie to the coming ambush.

In the distance he could hear the whine of the helicopter, but it did not seem to be moving closer. It could mean they'd spotted the flare but weren't going to risk Autie taking a shot at the aircraft by moving closer. He prayed they'd radioed Logan's position to a ground force. Help might be arriving any minute.

But he wasn't counting on it.

Even Autie with his formidable skills couldn't avoid making a whisper of noise as he climbed the path to Logan's position. The scrape of boots on the gravel floated up to Logan. He'd have to come up that path. All the other approaches would take him across deadly drops and cliffs that plunged into nowhere. And Autie would feel the pressure of time. With a chopper in the area, he'd have to complete his mission quickly.

Logan was relieved to hear the occasional sounds of Autie's progress. It meant he hadn't decided to go after Isabel. He knew if he failed, she'd be next.

Perhaps it would not be in these wasted acres. Maybe not

even in the upcoming months, but if Isabel was taken to safety, Autie would find her, Logan was sure of it. He wondered again what the man's motivation was and why he'd let Logan uncover the body of Nora Baker while he watched.

Was John Trigg in contact with Autie even now? Urging him on in his deadly pursuit? It seemed pointless. Logan could take no more time to muddle through the killer's motivations. Autie was close now, a few yards down the trail. The wind died away, leaving Logan tensed for the arrival of the man who sought to kill him.

Isabel registered only terror as the hands pushed her back toward the shelter of the rock. It was not Autie who half supported and half dragged her, but a slender man with dark eyes and dusky skin.

He said something that she could not understand through her fear.

Tank leaped into her lap and slavered his rubbery tongue over her face. Instinctively, she clasped him to her, still eyeing the stranger. "Who…?"

He uncapped a canteen and knelt next to her.

"Bill Cloudman. Bentley and his team are just west of our location."

Tank licked her enthusiastically.

Bill gently pushed him out of the way. "On my way here, I picked up Tank. He brought me in this direction. He's a good dog."

Isabel managed a smile. "So I've been told." She buried her head in the dog's fur for a moment, feeling the relief surge through her. Then she sipped from the offered canteen, the water cool and delicious on her dry tongue. She wanted to keep drinking, to let the liquid cool her insides, but she pushed it away.

"Logan."

Cloudman nodded. "I saw the signal flare. He's on the pinnacle. There." Bill pointed.

Isabel pushed Tank off her lap. "We've got to get to him. Autie's going to kill him."

Cloudman didn't answer, only nodded and stowed the canteen. She saw he had a gun in a holster at his belt. Though the baseball cap shadowed his face, his eyes glittered intensely from beneath the brim.

Cloudman leading, sticking to the shade as much as possible, they made their way to the base of the pinnacle, Tank running at Isabel's side.

Logan heard Autie stop just on the other side of the curve. He could almost hear the man's thoughts. He'd be thinking the same thing. Was it a trap? Was Logan waiting with a gun around the corner?

He savored the thought. Things might not work out the way he'd planned, but at least he'd turned the tables for a moment.

Then Autie moved forward, slowly, each footstep planted carefully, as though he was walking across slippery ground. Logan saw the first flicker of movement in the lenses of the sunglasses.

A little closer, he urged silently. *Just a few more steps.*

The end of Autie's rifle appeared in the reflection.

One step more.

Another small slice of what was coming and he had enough information.

Body tensed and ready, his legs propelled him forward at the exact time Autie emerged around the corner. He crashed into the rifle with all the strength left in him.

The shot rang through the air and Isabel screamed.

Bill unholstered his weapon and charged up the trail, Tank

outstripping him in a few strides. Isabel willed her legs to move up the steep trail, wondering with sick dread what they would find at the top.

If he was hurt…

If he was… She didn't allow herself to finish her thought. Her body screamed out for her to stop, but she would not. Not until she knew, one way or another.

As Logan and Autie fought for possession of the rifle, Logan's ears rang from the sound of the shot. Autie was strong, arms like steel as they grappled. Rolling around the trail loosened puffs of dust that whirled around them and stung their eyes.

With a vicious yank, Logan pulled the rifle free, but his hands were slick with sweat and the weapon skidded off the path and over the side of the pinnacle.

Autie scrambled back and got to his feet, breathing hard. "Why, Captain Price. Fancy meeting you here. Are you ready to die yet?"

Logan crouched in a ready position, arms raised defensively. "Not here. Not because of you."

Autie laughed as he removed a six-inch hunting knife from his belt. "It comes down to this. I will treat your death with honor, Captain, as a courtesy, you understand, for a fellow soldier and patriot."

The point of the knife blazed in the waning sunlight.

Autie circled the tip expertly. "I am sure that you were the recipient of a good deal of hand-to-hand combat training, were you not?"

"Plenty," Logan said as he pulled his own knife from the leather case on his hip. He'd begun to ease from foot to foot, gauging Autie's skill, sizing up the best way to attack and defend. Left, he would feint left. He tensed to attack when an unmistakable sound reached his ears. The tiny jingle of metal tags. He resisted the urge to smile. "There's just one favor I'd like to ask, one fellow soldier to another."

Autie frowned. "What is that?"

"Don't hurt the dog."

Autie raised a puzzled eyebrow as Tank barreled into view and sailed through the air, burying his teeth in Autie's wrist.

TWENTY TWO

Logan seized Autie's knife as the impact knocked it loose.

Bill turned Autie over and cuffed him with a pair of plastic restraints. When the dog continued to bark and snarl, Bill spoke a strange guttural word to the animal, who instantly sat.

Logan eyed the dog, amazed. "What language was that?"

"Lakota. Tank's bilingual of course, but Lakota is his primary language." Bill shot Logan an innocent look. "His language skills are strong."

"No wonder Tank never listens to me. Why didn't you tell me you trained him using Lakota?"

"Because your language skills are terrible." He hauled Autie to his feet.

Logan saw Isabel standing with her hands to her mouth, her face a ghastly white. He went to her. "It's okay now. It's over." He felt her body shudder as she sobbed onto his shirt front.

"I thought..." she started.

"Forget it. It's all over. We're going to get you out of here and have a doctor check you out."

She leaned against him and he traced circles on her back,

keeping her turned away from Autie. He had to strain to hear her when she spoke.

"But it's not over until we know who hired Autie to kill me and my sister."

Logan had nothing to say about that. He continued to hold her. All he could feel was a profound relief that she was alive.

Bentley and two men plowed around the corner, guns drawn. He took in the situation. "Glad to see no one is hurt."

"Isabel is," Logan snapped. "Autie grazed her shoulder with a bullet and she's dehydrated. We need to get her to a hospital."

Bill pushed Autie forward to Bentley. "Here's your man."

As Autie drew abreast of Logan he stopped. His face was sweat-stained and bleeding from a cut above the eye, but he did not appear to be a man who had been beaten. "As the great Custer himself might have said, I would be glad to see a battle every day during my life, with such a worthy opponent." He nodded his head. "You have been a challenging adversary and I am honored to be vanquished by a soldier of your caliber."

Logan could not keep the satisfaction out of his voice. "You're going to prison, Autie, like your father. I'm sure you'll find all kinds of worthy opponents there."

He smiled. "Perhaps you are right, Captain Price, but it is a very long way from here to prison. Who knows the twists and turns of fate that may occur in the length of that journey?"

Bill nudged him. "Don't worry. I'll make sure you get there safely."

Autie had almost passed Logan and Isabel when he lowered his voice and whispered. "Do give the general my sincerest and humble apologies for not carrying out her mission. I would apologize myself, but I am otherwise engaged."

Logan's heart thudded to a stop. *Her?*

Isabel's face mirrored his own shock.

Bill hadn't missed the pronoun either. "Go. There's another chopper on the way. I'll stay here with Tank and those two." He pointed to the cops who had arrived with Bentley. "You and Bentley see it through to the end."

Logan nodded. "Thank you, Bill."

"My pleasure."

Bentley peppered Logan with questions as they ran to the chopper, but Logan didn't answer any of them.

Isabel kept up well, but Logan still stopped once to insist that she drink and catch her breath. When they were strapped into the chopper the aircraft took off into a spectacular sunset.

He knew by Isabel's silence that she'd understood Autie's revelation. Her face was grave and she watched Logan closely, probably to see how he was reacting. He'd decided not to allow himself that luxury until they confronted her face-to-face.

"We'll take you to the hospital first." Logan started to speak to the chopper pilot but Isabel stopped him.

"No. We talk to her first."

"You need medical care."

"I need my sister's murderer caught."

He looked into her dark eyes, darker now against the pale cast of her face. "Are you sure, Isabel?"

She squeezed his hand in answer and he thought again that she was the bravest person he'd ever met.

The chopper delivered them back to the clearing where they'd started the trail ride. Most of the people were gone, but John was there, holding Blue Boy's reins. Isabel's smile at the sight of the horse was nothing short of spectacular. Next to John, sitting on a card chair with a phone pressed to her ear, was Sheila Trigg.

Logan headed straight for Sheila, with Bentley and Isabel struggling to keep up. At his approach, her face drained of color and she hung up the phone.

"Trying to get in touch with Autie?" Logan snapped.

"What?" She gave him a smile. "Silly boy. I don't know what you're talking about. We've been worried sick about you both. Are you all right? Are you hurt?"

Logan tried to hold his anger in check. "I think you know exactly what I'm talking about, Sheila."

Bentley cleared his throat. "We just took Autie into custody."

She kept up the facade for a moment, staring first at Bentley and then at Logan, until her face crumpled. Wrapping her arms tightly around herself, she blinked furiously.

John came over and handed the reins to Isabel without a word. "What's wrong, Mom?" He snarled at Bentley, "I told you to stay away from my mother."

Logan stared him down. "Your mother hired Autie to kill Cassie and Isabel."

John's mouth dropped open. Then he laughed. "You're really reaching now. You'd rather concoct this crazy story than face the facts about your girlfriend? Wise up before you lose what's left of your mind."

Bentley cut in, "Autie admitted it when we arrested him."

John snorted. "And you're going to trust the word of some lunatic?"

"We're going to believe it, because he's telling the truth," Logan said, his eyes on Sheila. "That day at the ranch, you said you saw Autie watching me clear the ravine before you fell. I couldn't figure out why he would stand out in the open, allowing me to unearth the body. Truth was, he wouldn't. He wasn't there. We'd just discovered his hunting blind and I winged him in the shoulder. He was holed up somewhere else."

Sheila shook her head. "I don't understand."

"Yes, you do." Isabel spoke softly, but they all turned to

look at her. "You said you were a social worker once upon a time, and Bill Cloudman told us social services tried to work with Autie's family before his mom was murdered. That's how you knew him, wasn't it? You'd visited his family."

"No," Sheila said, struggling to her feet.

Isabel stroked Blue Boy as she continued. "John killed Nora and couldn't face the consequences, so you stepped in to save him. I think you didn't want my sister to discover Nora's body. When she started on her plans to have Logan clear the ravine, you panicked and hired Autie to kill her. You're so desperate to protect John that you killed my sister."

John lunged forward, but Logan pushed him back.

In the midst of John's heavy breathing he almost missed Sheila's answer.

"Not John," Sheila said, her voice quivering. "Not John. Carl."

Even John sucked in a breath at Sheila's words. "Mom, what are you talking about? Tell them this is ridiculous. Tell them."

She shook her head, eyes riveted to a spot on the ground. "I didn't want you to know. Ever. Things started to snowball, one after the other until the whole situation was surreal, like a horrible low-budget movie. I tried to stop it, but I couldn't."

Logan's mind reeled. Carl? He couldn't take it all in. "Carl killed Nora Baker?"

Sheila nodded, speaking as if she were in a trance. "He was trying to persuade her to leave town because I told him to. Because I knew she wasn't right for John. She was a gold digger, nothing more." She looked up into the face of her son. "But you couldn't see it. You wouldn't see it, so I asked Carl to give her a ride home after work one night and offer her money to leave town. The stupid girl threw a fit and refused. She got out of the car and stalked off. Carl tried to catch up with her and accidentally hit her with the car."

Bentley shifted. "Carl killed Nora Baker?"

"Yes. And then he panicked and pushed her body into the ravine. He knocked loose a few stones and caused a rock slide. I don't know what the fool was thinking."

John's face had gone milk-white. "Dad killed Nora. And you hired Autie to make sure Cassie didn't unearth her body."

"Cassie refused to give up her plans to clear that ravine. We even offered to buy her property, but she turned that down, too. I hired Autie to persuade her, but she fought him and he killed her. Then Isabel arrived." Sheila looked at her. "I figured you would be happy to unload the ranch, or before you arrived we'd have some time to unearth the body." She pressed a hand to her temple. "If only Carl hadn't been so stupid. He's been so wracked with guilt since he killed the girl, he's started drinking too much."

Logan remembered Carl's emotional outburst at Mountain Cloud.

It never should have happened to her. She was young and had her whole life to go yet. If Logan had only guessed Carl was talking about Nora Baker, the woman he killed.

"I thought Dad was drinking because he discovered your affair with Bentley," John said.

Bentley flinched.

Logan pressed her. "It was your decision to keep Autie on the payroll to scare Isabel off the ranch, or kill her if she refused to go."

Sheila sighed. "After the body was discovered, I tried to call Autie off, but I couldn't reach him. He's like a lion with a carcass. Once he starts something, he'll never stop."

"So Autie killed my sister and almost killed Logan and me because you paid him to?" Isabel asked.

Sheila hesitated. "I guess it doesn't matter now. Autie took the money, but I also promised him once Carl was elected to the Senate, he would help get Oscar out of jail somehow."

Logan shook his head. "Fat chance of that happening."

Sheila shrugged. "Autie's smart. He probably figured Carl could at least get some kind of inside information to get Oscar moved or transferred someplace where Autie could help him escape." She groaned. "All this work, all the years of smiling and glad-handing a bunch of ignorant townspeople, kissing babies and eating casseroles. Now it's all for nothing."

John stepped close to her. "And that's really what this is all about, isn't it, Mom? It's about getting Dad elected so you could finally be a senator's wife."

She shook her head, a pleading look on her face. "No. No, I wanted Nora gone to protect you, and the other things…just happened."

"You wanted Nora gone because she wasn't suitable, and you helped cover up the crime because you wanted to save Dad's career." He spat out the words. "You had Cassie killed because of your own ambition. I loved her, and you had her killed."

She held out a hand. "No, it wasn't like that, please, honey."

"It was exactly like that. It's always been like that. You've never been happy as a rancher's wife or a rancher's mother. That's why you pushed Dad into politics, that's why you shoved me into law school and that's why…" His voice broke. "You're responsible for killing the only two women I ever loved."

Sheila's mouth moved but she didn't speak.

John turned to Logan and Isabel, a look of utter defeat on his face. "I'm sorry. I was wrong about everything." He stroked the horse tenderly and walked away.

"Wait, John," Sheila cried. "I'm so sorry, honey. Please don't leave. I need to make you understand."

John continued on until he was swallowed up by the darkness.

She looked at Logan. "I'm so sorry."

"Me, too, Sheila," Logan said. "I trusted you both and we almost died for it."

With a pained look on his face, Bentley pulled Sheila's arms behind her back and snapped the handcuffs into place.

Isabel made sure Blue Boy was settled comfortably into the barn with extra feed and a blanket, along with Echo and Striker, who had been brought home by the Moonlight Ride volunteers. They'd left a note tacked to the front door that, in spite of everything, the Quinns wanted to discuss buying the horses when Isabel was feeling up to it.

The bandage applied by a chagrined Dr. Lunardi at the clinic chafed against her sleeve. He hadn't exactly apologized for missing the real cause of Cassie's death, but he took gentle care in cleaning her wound.

Despite her meticulous attention to the exhausted Blue Boy, she returned twice that night to check on him, passing by Logan's trailer. The second time she'd heard him on the phone. She knew he was making preparations to leave.

She wasn't sure why he hadn't already taken the trailer back, since Autie was arrested and Carl and Sheila Trigg were, too. He loved her, she knew, and the thought brought her a bittersweet comfort. She would have that to hold on to for the rest of her life. He loved her and she loved him, but love didn't always keep two people together.

Poor John, she thought as she sat sipping tea in the front room of the tiny house, waiting for the sun to rise. He really had loved Cassie. Maybe if things had been different, she would have grown to love him, too, and they could have settled down and made Cassie's dream come true together.

The sky swirled with a myriad of purples and reds.

If she could bottle this moment, the perfect sunrise, the stirring of the horses in the stable, the nearness of a man she loved desperately, if she could gather it all into a place where she could draw the feelings out and steep herself in them, she knew she could find joy in each day God had in store for her.

The knock at the door didn't startle her. It seemed as though all her fears had been left behind in the Badlands. She found Logan on the step.

"Morning. I saw the light on. Figured you were up." He avoided looking at her, hands shoved into his pockets.

"Come in for some coffee."

He followed her into the kitchen. "Feeling okay?"

"Sore and banged up, but the hot shower was better than any medicine. Where's Tank?"

"With Bill." He chuckled, turning the mug in his hands. "I'm gonna miss that dog."

She blinked. "Bill's going to keep him?"

Logan nodded and she thought she saw a tiny quiver in his mouth. "Yeah, Bill's his master, really, and Tank loves him. Dog's good for Bill. He only gave him to me on loan while he got his head together after his partner's death."

She sighed. "Tank loves you, too."

He took a breath. "All for the best, anyway."

It was. He wouldn't be able to take Tank with him back to the Air Force. God was tending to all the details for Logan to leave. Her heart squeezed. "I'm glad it's all working out."

"Look." He let out a sigh. "I need to apologize to you. I thought I knew the Triggs. I really never conceived they were capable of what they did. I was blinded by my friendship with them."

"No need for an apology. Even their son had no idea."

"I believed them and it put you in danger. I'm sorry."

She wanted to erase his sorrow. "Really, there's no way you could have known. Don't punish yourself." She handed him some coffee. "The Quinns want to take the horses."

"That's great," he said, voice flat.

She took a deep breath. Saying it out loud for the first time would make it real. "But I'm not going to let them."

He stopped with the coffee cup halfway to his mouth. "Why?"

"I've decided to stay here and keep the ranch. I'm going to make it what Cassie wanted it to be."

His looked shifted from amazement to concern. "You don't have to do that, just because of everything that's happened."

"I know. It's not out of guilt. I love the horses and I feel like I've been given a gift, a dream that I can embrace, a place where I finally belong. Too bad I had to find that out the hard way." She tried a laugh, but his face was so serious. "Logan, what are you thinking?"

He put the cup down carefully. "I'm thinking that I'm the luckiest man in South Dakota."

"What do you mean?"

"I made a phone call." He cleared his throat. "I turned down the trainer job."

She gasped. "Why? It's your dream."

"It started out that way. When I was injured, I couldn't accept it. I focused my entire life on getting back what I felt was taken from me. Until now."

She was too confused to speak.

The excitement in his voice was electric, his eyes shone. "It took being lost in the Badlands and being almost blown up and watching you suffer so badly to open my eyes, but now I finally see it. I didn't want to trust again after Nancy, didn't want to take responsibility for my failings, but I've got a new dream now, and it's better than anything I've ever imagined."

Hardly daring to believe it, Isabel whispered, "Tell me, Logan."

He took her hands in his. "I've decided to stay here, to

really commit my whole heart to this wild state. Maybe I'll make the contractor business work, or maybe I'll find something else to do, but I'm not going back to pararescue. I was hoping I could change your mind about going back to L.A."

His hands were warm, face close to hers.

"And there's one more thing, the most important thing. God showed this stubborn solider the blessing he had right before his eyes. I love you, Isabel. I love you like I've never loved anyone or anything in this entire crazy world. I want us to get married and build a life together. If that means helping you run this ranch, then I'll sign on for that, too."

"But…" she managed. "You—you said you'd rather ride a tank than a horse."

He grinned. "Did I ever tell you my nickname? The one I got from the guys on my squad?"

"No."

He laughed. "They called me Cowboy. Now if that isn't a sign that I should learn to love those ridiculous animals, I don't know what is."

She pulled away, body shivering, hands pressed to her flushed cheeks.

Logan moved to her. "What is it? Did I move too fast? Did I misunderstand?"

Through her tears she saw his face, lined with worry, scraped and bruised from their adventure, the perfect face. "I love you, too. So much. Forever."

The smile lit up his eyes as he bent to kiss her.

* * * * *

Dear Reader,

The Badlands of South Dakota appear to be a desolate place, harsh and unforgiving. It is here that Logan and Isabel will fight for survival against a man who wants them both to disappear. But the Badlands are also a place filled with life, an environment so completely unique that it proves to be a crucible where Isabel and Logan will discover the essence of who God meant them to be.

As I researched this area, I was amazed at the way God created such a breathtaking landscape and uniquely fashioned his creatures to flourish there. It reminded me that we are designed by Him to live here, to lift each other up and walk through this dangerous world together, under His watchful eye.

Thank you for taking your time to read this book. I pray you will find it entertaining and uplifting. I treasure contact with my readers. If you would like to send a comment or question, please visit my Web site at www.danamentink.com.

Fondly,

Dana Mentink

QUESTIONS FOR DISCUSSION

1. Isabel regrets her strained relationship with her sister. Why is it sometimes harder to mend broken relationships with family than with friends and acquaintances?

2. The bond between animal and human can be a strong one. Do you have an animal that has enriched your life?

3. Logan helped Cassie's mother, a complete stranger. Have you ever received help from someone you didn't know? How did they reach out to you?

4. Autie says, "The truth will hang around your neck like the heaviest of stones." How would Autie's worldview be different if he accepted Jesus as his savior?

5. Logan prays, "Lord, You know that's the answer for me." What do you think about Logan's prayer?

6. Nancy's betrayal hurt Logan deeply. Have you ever experienced betrayal? Were you able to overcome the hurt? How?

7. Both Logan and Isabel made choices that pulled them away from God. How can we know if our own choices are staying within the boundaries of God's plan for us?

8. Logan feels that horses are more humane than humans, in the way they integrate outsiders into their world. What do you think about this statement?

9. Isabel comes to believe that if you keep people shut out,

you pay a terrible price. What are the ways we keep other people at arm's length?

10. What do you feel is your God-given mission in your own corner of the world?

11. Will Isabel be able to make peace with the loss of her sister? Why or why not?

12. How can our relationship with God help us reconcile unresolved conflicts in our lives?

13. What challenges are ahead for Logan and Isabel?